RISE FROM RUIN
Guardians of the Fae Realms: Book 14
JL Madore

JL Madore

Cover Design: Gombar Cover Designs

Note: The moral right of the author has been asserted.

Rise from Ruin : Guardians of the Fae Realms

JL Madore -- 1st ed.

ISBN: 978-1-998372-71-3

CHAPTER ONE

Lark

*I*t's said that in moments of extreme danger, your life flashes before your eyes. I'm not sure how dire that danger has to be because I've got nothing. With possibly twenty-six enemy super soldiers bearing down on us, my mental viewscreen is showing me nothing except the flashing lights of the bunker's alarm and the worried faces of the seven men around me.

"How many?" Mac snaps, ejecting the magazine of his gun to check his ammunition.

"I have sixteen entering the warehouse up top," Link says, his fingers dancing across the interface console. "Four standing guard. Twelve advancing."

"So, only a dozen super soldiers closing in to kill us," Lukas gripes. "And here I was, almost worried." He fusses with his tactical watch, cursing, and then pulls out his phone. "Communications are down."

Mac grunts, raking rough fingers through his russet hair as he watches the numbers of the elevator tick off as it's called to the surface. Other than his free-flowing red waves hanging to his shoulders, Mac is all military might. He's built and skilled and so damned confident in a crisis I'd actually believe he might not be afraid of anything.

"Wait! What about Alpha and Beta?" I ask, glancing at Flash. "They are still in their stasis cylinders on the fourth floor. How long would it take to power them up to help us?"

Flash frowns, his expression tightening as he tilts his head. "Power them up?"

I wince. "I'm sorry. That was insensitive. I meant to say activate them... you know, bring them online to help us."

Lukas holds up a hand. "And before you do that, can we be certain they would even be on our side?"

Link throws Lukas a dirty look. "They would be on the side of surviving and working with us. I can't say if that is on *your* side, but it is on ours."

Flash lets off a throaty grumble at his brother. "We are all on the *same* side, Link. And to answer your question, my lovely, they will be quick to engage. Link has initiated their waking sequence."

Lukas' head swings around on a pivot, his eyes wide. "You did *what?*"

Link flicks his hand in the air, his attention still focused on the interface console. "Yes, I took the initiative to release our brothers from the torment of endless night. You're welcome. They might be the added force needed to save your lives."

Lukas doesn't look like that makes him any less angry. Dune grips Lukas' arm and gives it a squeeze. "That's an argument for later, magic man. One we might not even have to worry about if we don't get out of here."

"They're in the elevator," Link says, his hands moving at a blurring speed.

All conversation stops as the elevator lets off a sing-songy *bing* and I jog over to see what's happening. Two soldiers remain in the elevator car while ten exit onto the first floor and spread out.

"Are they looking for us?" I ask.

"Considering that they just opened those desk drawers, I'm going to say no," Dune says.

We watch the monitor as the team spreads out and searches the floor before making their way back and gathering in the elevator once more.

The elevator mechanics hum in the shaft and the soldiers descend until the quiet *bing* signals their arrival on the second floor.

We watch as they repeat the same process. Ten soldiers spill out onto the third floor while two remain inside and secure the elevator.

That makes no sense to me. "If they're not here for us, what are they searching for?"

Lukas frowns. "I think we're likely on the list, but yeah, what *else* are they searching for?"

"And why stop one floor at a time? If we can tap into the feeds and see them, surely they can tap into the feeds from up top and see we're down here."

Shift nods. "Likely so, but if they come straight down to the fifth floor and we have someone on two or possibly three, we could slip past them and escape or double back."

Mac nods. "Aye, maybe or maybe they're after somethin' besides us."

Tundra leans in to look at the screen and frowns. "And by them sending a dozen soldiers to fetch it, I assume it's important to them."

"What could be here that they need?" I ask, glancing around at the three. They may never have ventured to the other floors in the decade since their creation, but they are linked into the server system for the bunker and might know.

Flash meets my gaze, protective fury smoldering in his warm honey-gold eyes. "Two and three are the science labs."

"So, what are they after?"

"Maybe Andras Brass left an experiment incubating and forgot about it," Mac says.

"More likely they are after the serums," Link says.

I shake my head. "The serum to stabilize the emotions of the phase three soldiers?"

"Or the immobilization serum," Shift adds.

I blink as my mind catches up on that. "They have a take-down serum?"

"Of course," Lukas says, catching on. "If I'm Brass and my scientists and I live deep in a bunker with thirty genetically modified beings who are physically and militarily superior to us, we'd want a way to take them down if something goes wrong and they go rogue."

I grin. "Excellent. Then where is it and how do we get our hands on it?"

"There is no record in the system of where Brass and his team kept it," Link says.

"There wouldn't be," Shift adds. "Andras Brass has a lot of negative traits, but careless stupidity isn't one of them. He knows we can interface with the computer systems. Why would they document the one thing that could save them in a moment of life or death?"

Good point. "All right, so he's sent his army to descend floor by floor, and collect the serum they need to keep control of their soldiers."

Lukas grunts. "If it is the takedown serum, they can't know what it is, or they'd never get it for him."

"He wouldn't want to risk us finding it," Tundra says. "What good is it to have an army of super soldiers if the people you stole them from have a way to stop them?"

"So they come back to collect it," I say.

"But even if they found what they were looking for on one and two, they don't have all of it," Dune adds. "Because if things go badly, would you put your only chance for survival in one spot? I would keep it where I live, where I'm testing, and where I'm training the soldiers."

"That's the first, second, fourth, and fifth floors," Flash says.

"Weel, then I guess we've got a hunt ahead of us," Mac says, helping Lukas drag our dining table away from the wall to tip it as a shield for cover.

"But if they lived here, they could've grabbed it easily when they evacuated," Flash says.

"So, four is our best chance," I say.

Lukas shakes his head. "We increase our odds if we search two floors."

Mac grunts. "These floors are locked off from one another. According to the schematics, the elevator is the only way in or out, and the soldiers on the elevator won't want to share."

"But if they are searching each floor, one at a time, we might have time to get to the fourth before they do," I say.

Link's attention veers from the interface console to meet mine across the bunker living room. "And that would allow us the opportunity to engage Alpha and Beta."

The sing-songy *bing* of the elevator counting down another floor makes me jump. "They're on the third floor. It'll have to be now or never if we're doing this."

Link stands and scans the group. "Flash and Shift. You are with me."

"Like hell," Lukas snaps, raising his hand. "You don't call the shots here, buddy, and I am definitely not allowing the three super soldiers we have to go pick up two more and leave us in the dust."

Link frowns. "Strategically, if they are searching each floor in numerical order, having the strongest force to face them on four is the tactically sound decision. To divide us is to weaken our position."

Lukas shakes his head. "Not happening. You, Shift, Tundra, and Dune, up to four. Flash, Lark, Mac, and I will search this floor and get ready for the attack."

Flash raises a hand to stop Link from arguing. "It is an acceptable compromise. I will stay and help search this floor. Now go. There is no time to lose evaluating one another's male genitalia."

Lukas' face screws up and I bust out laughing. "I think he's saying measuring your dicks."

Mac curses, but the upturn of his mouth as he rubs his hand over his stubbled jaw suggests he found it funny, too. "All right. Let's get these doors open so ye can fly up there."

From that moment, there is no more talk.

Flash, Mac, and I pull back the elevator doors, and then Link, Shift, Tundra, and Dune launch up the elevator shaft. Lukas has taken control of the console and is trying to lock out the elevator controls long enough for the four of them to get the doors open on four and to get onto the floor safely.

Leaning into the dark cavity, I watch until the last tips of their wings disappear onto the floor above us. "They made it."

Flash and I ease back and let the doors close.

"Now to search for the takedown serum," I say, turning to assess our living space with fresh eyes. "What do you think we're looking for?"

Lukas finishes whatever override protocols he's trying to lock down the elevator and then joins Mac, Flash, and me on the hunt. "Probably a tranq gun of some kind. If I was Brass planning for this, I'd want a delivery method that allowed me to take them down without getting too close."

"That would ensure the greatest odds of survival," Flash says, agreeing with him.

The four of us spread out, and the search begins.

Lukas pulls open the cabinet doors and drawers in the kitchen. Mac disappears into the training room. And Flash and I pull the couches away from the wall and yank the artwork down, hoping to find a safe.

That we're trashing the place searching for takedown tranqs that may or may not exist before we're overrun by a super soldier death squad is almost comical—or it would be without the 'death squad' part—or the fact that any of this is real.

"Mac, see if there's anything in there we can use in a fight," Lukas shouts, moving from the kitchen counters over to the appliances.

"I doubt wooden swords will be effective against them, but—"

The *bing* of the elevator stops us all for the heartbeat it takes to wish the others well. "Fourth floor."

Flash nods. "We shall do them the highest honor by finding what we're looking for and getting out of here alive."

Mac joins us carrying a medicine ball in each hand and tilts his head back the way he came. "Bring the metal dumbbells, will ye? I figure ye can throw them like hardballs."

Flash rushes off to do as he's asked and returns a moment later carrying the entire collection of hand weights in their stand. He sets them down behind the upturned dining table and then gestures toward the bedroom corridor. "Shall we?"

I've pulled up the living room rug, searching for a trapdoor, and found nothing. "Yeah, sure—"

The thundering *tat-a-tat-a-tat* of automatic gunfire sounds off above our heads and I suck in a breath. Our bond is very new, but I care about those boys.

I read the same concern on Mac's face as well.

And unlike the five of us exploring the beginnings of what me being their catalyst means, Lukas is fully bonded and mated with Tundra and Dune.

He must be losing his mind.

"And what's the plan when we take these assholes down?" I ask, jogging with Flash toward the bedrooms.

"Och, that's easy, lass. We kick ass, get clear of this cluster fuck, and then we meet up back at the burned-out barn."

"Thornebane Castle offers a better defensive position," Lukas shouts from somewhere down the hall...

The washroom maybe?

Mac pulls the tipped dining table closer to where Flash set the hand weights by the corridor into the barracks. "Aye, but leadin' this shit show of an offensive force straight to yer family would be a mistake."

Lukas curses and Flash tugs me toward his room. "I'll use the desk interface console in my quarters to send a message to the Amberloq central command. No matter what happens here, we should warn them about what they're up against."

"You can do that?" Lukas snaps.

"I should think so. Valorous made it standard protocol to have the security of her base buildings hard-wired through to the Amberloq command."

Lukas nods. "Then yes, if they haven't already disabled that access, give them our sit rep and tell them we're trapped."

Flash grabs my wrist and I'm tugged along in his wake. When we arrive at the doorway to his quarters, I grab the door frame and pull back. "Flash, sweetie, stop! I need to keep searching."

He sends me an apologetic smile. "You are brave and have an inextinguishable fire in you, my lovely, but you are no match for what comes. I need you to stay with me so I can ensure your safety."

Ouch. Tell me how you really feel.

With him holding my arm, there's no way the emotional receptors of his gift missed the sting of how his words slapped me. He steps closer and presses a warm palm to my cheek. "Apologies. My programming has yet to compensate for my possessive need to protect you. Please stay with me while I focus on my task."

I want to tell him how many things are wrong with that—to stand my ground—but now is not the time. And while it hurts my pride to be found lacking in my ability to take on a hostile force, he's not wrong.

Especially when that hostile force is an army of genetically modified super soldiers.

"Fine. Do your thing. I'll grab my gun from my room and join you in thirty seconds."

He looks like he might protest, but there's no time. I give him a gentle push toward his room. "I'm only one room down the hall, Flash. You'll hear if the elevator chimes and you're closer to the incoming soldiers than me. If you need to be at my side, you will be, I promise."

My argument must hold water because he nods and rushes toward his desk.

I run to the next room down the hall and grab the gun Mac assigned me the other day when this mission began. Has it seriously only been a couple of days?

Wow. My mind flashes through those moments at triple speed. Coming to this bunker to secure the genetically modified super soldiers Honor's aunt created to strengthen her military force... the battle Connor Mac and I fought against three naked men... how my blood acted as their catalyst to activate their genetic enhancements... how Mac and I have been drawn into a sexual if not personal relationship with them...

It's been a whirlwind.

And while the terms 'fated mates' and 'soul seared' are well-known and respected events that could explain this, as far as I know, 'catalyst lover' has never come into play in the Fae Realm.

Pulling open the side table drawer, the closet, and the desk reveals nothing. Before we got here, this was Andras Brass's room, so if the big mad scientist lived in this space, I would've expected him to keep protection close at hand.

Unless he took it with him when he evacuated.

Dammit, that's a possibility too.

Still, this room holds the largest probability of finding what we need to get out of this. Lying on my back, I put myself in the place of Andras Brass. "So, I'm in here, sleeping, and I hear a commotion—a struggle out in the living area... Where the hell is my weapon?"

CHAPTER TWO

Link

From the moment we leave Flash and Lady Lark downstairs, I feel their absence. Logically, it makes no sense because Lukas wasn't wrong. When I suggested that my brothers and I venture up here to awaken Alpha and Beta, I had every intention of procuring our freedom and leaving this bunker and everything it represents behind us.

But now, at least for the moment, that is not possible. And while I'd like to say that the only thing stopping us is the separation between us and Flash, the truth is my mind is very much taken up with concerns for our catalyst, Lady Lark, as well.

The four of us speak little as we race through the administrative space near the elevators and stride deeper into the fourth floor.

I can't believe that it has been a mere eighty-three hours and seventeen minutes since Connor Mac and Lady Lark first engaged with us.

As we pass through the antechamber room where the five of us fought, I can't help but replay that moment in my mind.

Driven to survive and protect this bunker, I was ill-prepared for the potency of Lark's blood on my lip. One drop of blood changed the course of everything we had known until that date.

No one can say now that we are defective.

The only thing that was ever defective was the assumptions of the scientific team that deemed us a failed experiment.

"I take it you boys are going to handle updating your friends on the situation?" Dune asks.

"We shall," Shift says.

"Then we'll look around for the serums. If you hear gunfire or screaming for help, jump in and do your super soldier thing to save our butts."

Tundra, the tall, ebony-haired one with the glorious white wings, scoffs. "The battle hasn't even begun and you have us getting our asses kicked?"

Dune flashes his mate a saucy look. "You and I are badass, Frosty, but us against eight super soldiers will not end well. There's no way around it."

Tundra chuckles. "Since when did you become the grown-up?"

"I know, right? I blame all the sex. You, Lukas, and Shadow are infusing me with wisdom and maturity."

"And yet, that comment just proved how wrong you are." The two of them rush off in different directions, hoping to find something to be used to fend off the incoming force.

Shift and I rush straight back to where our brothers remain in their stasis cylinders. The moment I access the interface console and activate their programming, I instruct them to wake up ready to engage.

Alpha and Beta are not like my brothers and me. Their design centered heavily on physical superiority: speed, strength, and an almost indestructible durability. What the scientists soon realized was that no matter what amount of training they received, the insufficiencies in the design scope of their physical appearance and social understanding meant they could never blend in among the people of Dornte.

In their minds, we were to be built to not only fight and protect the people of the quadrant but to live among them undetected in the instances when spying on them was necessary.

And so Alpha and Beta were cast to the side.

"Wake, my brothers, for it is time to fight for our survival."

Alpha's eyelids open, his programming still updating behind the retinal coloration of his ocular units. Pale blue data cycles past the slate grey of his pupils, and then he tilts his head and regards me. "Fighting for our survival. Who is our enemy, brother?"

"The third-generation soldiers created in this facility have gone rogue with the scientist, Andras Brass. He has ordered them to eliminate us as their opposing force and to keep them for himself instead of for our directive purpose of protecting Dornte in the name of the Thornebane royalty."

Beta awakens and joins his brother, stepping out of his stasis cylinder and surveying his surroundings. "I also sense Elbirfae and humans within the bunker."

"They are with us," Shift says. "The female is our catalyst and the male who transforms is mine. They are to be protected at all costs."

Beta cants his head to the side, absorbing information. "And the other human?"

"He is Princess Honor's mate and a Guardian of the Crown."

"As are the two male Elbirfae on this floor," I add.

Shift nods and hands each of the males a pair of pants from the shelf. "The Elbirfae are the current Biome Generals, here to assess our worthiness to join the Amberloq. This is our chance to prove ourselves."

Alpha's processing completes, and he focuses his gaze on me.

"And the other soldiers wish to keep us from being given our opportunity."

"That is correct."

Alpha nods. "Then we will fight for our princess, her mates, and our Biome Generals."

"We are pleased to add your might to our force, my brothers," Shift says.

I'm not pleased Shift tied our loyalty to the crown of Dornte, but for the moment, the important thing is that Alpha and Beta understand what side they are on and what we face.

"There are ten, possibly twelve, generation three soldiers about to breach this floor. Our aim is clear. We will survive and eliminate the opposing force, proving our worth as defenders of Dornte."

"And is lethal force approved?" Beta asks, stepping into the pants and securing the waistband at his hips.

Technically, it was never discussed, but I feel confident in answering that. "Yes."

Shift pulls off his shirt and releases his wings. "Our time is now, brothers. Strength be with you."

"And with you," we all say.

The high-pitched chime of the elevator arriving at our floor brings with it a rush of excitement and a clarity of purpose. We have waited twelve years to prove our mettle. Our time is now.

Shift

I SEE the glimmer of fire burning in Link's gaze and feel his excitement bursting over our connection. *This is it, my brother, our moment to prove that we were never defective—their assessment of our worth was.*

Agreed.

The metallic rumblings of the elevator deliver the enemy to the floor, and we rush to greet them. The offensive force advances, striking hard and fast. Armed with automatic weapons, they spray the air with a liberal wash of bullets.

It is a futile first attack, considering our wings are as bullet-proof as those of the Elbirfae warriors we were created to fight with. I curl my wings around me as I advance, marching forward with heavy footsteps, cutting the distance between me and our foe.

Despite the preliminary impression of might, I realize the elevator has hemorrhaged a motley crew of goblins, elves, nymphs, shifters, and faery, all wearing black tactical clothing.

Ah, yes. Lukas mentioned the third generation of soldiers were constructed from the shells of citizens.

While they might be equipped with Brass' latest technology, they in no way create a visual image of a fighting unit like my brothers and me.

I take a deep breath, focus on the nearest opponent, and lock eyes with a man with a scar running through the line of his brow. Overconfident, he reaches for me as if to force me into action.

Does he truly believe I am inferior?

If his briefing came from Brass, then yes, he does. All the more to my advantage.

The male's charge is strong, his weapon poised, but I am not defenseless to his attack. Rushing in low, I grip the shaft of the gun, force the aim off to the side, and bring my knee up to connect with his ribs.

The hit is solid, and the force of the blow makes him stagger to steady his balance. His eyes flare with both shock and indignation that my strike hit home.

Before he has time to recover, I reclaim his wrist and turn, ducking under his arm to straighten behind his back. I am about to snap his elbow joint when a second opponent—a female elf with black skin—rushes into our battle and swings a powerful fist toward my head.

With no freehand to raise a block, I thrust my wing forward to catch her downward thrust. Her assault shifts and I spin to put the man in my grasp between us as a shield.

The female's strike lands with a violent crunch on the man's face. The crack of cartilage and possibly cheekbone echoes around us and I find the spray of blood in the air to be most satisfying.

The female shows no sign of regret for the damage she caused her comrade, for without a beat of hesitation, she unsheathes two wicked sharp daggers and slices the air between us.

Her swing is too fast to track... even with my heightened reflexes.

The sting of the blade through my flesh draws a line of blood from my shoulder to just below my collarbone. It is a surface wound and doesn't affect any of my primary functions.

At least until her other hand moves in, unseen from below. The point of the blade penetrates deeply and I activate a self-diagnostic of the damage.

The male takes my momentary distraction and capitalizes on his opportunity. He drives a steel fist into the tender flesh at the small of my back.

Bending forward, I thrust a kick behind me and take out his knee while yanking the blade from my body.

A grunt of aggravated surprise escapes from the female, as I barrel forward and land a swiping gash across her hip. She spins, her dark eyes storming.

Gripping the edge of a lab table, she screams as she hurls it through the air at me. The dagger clangs to the floor before I get my hands up to brace for the impact.

Instead of catching the flying furniture, I redirect it and send it soaring at the male about to close in on Tundra, the white-winged warrior.

During the moment I take to twist and divert the projectile, the male I've been fighting catches me in the temple with a solid strike.

My perception receptors are knocked temporarily offline and my vision goes dark.

The female rushes me and we end up in a scramble on the floor. I target her wounded hip as we roll, and she twists to escape my follow-up blows.

Unfortunately, without the specifications of these soldiers, I am fighting without knowledge of this female's weaknesses.

Beheading would certainly stop her. But short of decapitation, this is a learning moment.

Not that I am opposed to learning...

In truth, I relish the input. Twelve years of stasis has left me hungry for new experiences.

As she strikes out with her weapons, I grab the arm of the male soldier and pull him in to once again use him as my shield. He wrenches himself free and manages a solid kick to my stomach, knocking me to the floor.

Impressive. Their strength is noteworthy.

The force of the strike causes my body to skate across the floor on my backside. The discarded gun comes into view and I roll to claim the weapon.

The ineffectiveness of a gun against one of us notwithstanding, perhaps I can use it to hold them back while I seek a new opening for attack.

A thunderous crash to my left brings Link and two others into play. I dive out of the way and reclaim my footing as they take out a section of wall and crash into the laboratory beyond.

Spinning back to my opponents, I grip the weapon, surprised when the action halts their advance. *Curious.*

Firing the weapon sends an unpleasant vibration up my arms and through my shoulders.

I much prefer daggers.

The weapon has given them pause… and more.

When the male stiffens and drops to the ground, I'm puzzled. When the female does as well, I'm genuinely confused. I step closer and scan their vital signs.

They are offline.

I study my surroundings to find my brothers and the Elbirfae warriors in full battle and paying no attention. *Link? Flash? I believe their weapons are treated with the takedown serum we seek. I shot two, and they have fallen inactive and are reading as offline.*

Then, by all means, rain a storm of bullets upon them.

"Dune! Tundra! Disarm your opponents and turn the guns against them. They are the weapons you need and I don't think you will be affected."

"Yee-fucking-haw, blondie. Good to know."

I don't know Dune well, but find him to be a very strange fellow.

That is a thought for another moment.

Now is the time to turn the tables.

CHAPTER THREE

Flash

*a*fter I finish sending our situation report to the Amberloq central command computer, I push off the console at my desk and it's just as Lark said... I am closer to the incoming force than she is. Racing down the hall to her room, I rush in to secure her and — "What are you doing? Does your system need to recharge?"

Lark is on the bed, lying on her back, her hands stretched over her head.

"No," she grunts, reaching. "I'm not recharging."

She's running her hands along the crack between the mattress and the wall. The position elongates her torso, lifting the bottom edge of her shirt to expose her navel and ribs.

I scan the tantalizing band of bare skin. From this angle, her breasts look even more delicious than usual. "Is this sexual?" *It seems sexual.* "I applaud the idea, but there is no time, my lovely."

Lark is off the bed and chuckling. "No, sweet man. Not sexual. I was testing where Brass could reach if he was sleeping and attacked."

Oh, that makes sense. I reach behind my back, pull at the collar of my shirt, and toss the flimsy cotton covering onto her bed. Rolling my shoulders, I release my wings and am ready for the battle to come.

The pupils of her bright green eyes dilate as my wings unfurl, and she sucks in a breath. She traps her bottom lip between her teeth as her gaze roams hot over my skin.

I capture a section of her ebony hair and brush it behind her ear. I lean close to her cheek and caress her skin with my lips. "I wish I had the time to properly address your interests."

Her fingers trace down the ridged lines of my torso, and then her body sways closer to mine. "I do too. Be safe, sweet man."

I wrap my arms around her shoulders and press my lips to her forehead. "You as well."

The neuro-link I share with Link and Shift opens.

Link? Flash? I believe their weapons are treated with the takedown serum we seek. I shot two, and they have fallen inactive and are reading as offline.

Then, by all means, rain a storm of bullets upon them, Link replies.

With his message conveyed, Shift releases the connection and my mind falls silent as a second rhythmic thundering of bullets echoes above our heads.

My gaze falls upon the blanket of concern covering Lark's face. "Flash, what is it? Are you all right? What's happening?"

It means more to me than I can ever express that she cares. In all the years we've been inactive and forgotten, no one gave our well-being a second thought.

I press a gentle hand against the pulse racing at the side of her smooth neck. She knows the connection of flesh-on-flesh allows me to read her emotions, and she trusts me enough now that she doesn't mind the intrusion of her privacy.

More importantly, she sends me a rush of affection. "Shift

informed me he confiscated an assault weapon the generation three soldiers brought to take us down. He believes the ammunition is treated with the serum we seek because he fired it upon two of the soldiers and rendered them disabled."

Lark's bright green eyes flare with excitement. "Perfect. Then stay behind me. I don't want you to be hit by any of those bullets."

As she moves to pass, my confusion increases. "Wait. No, I... How did this become about you protecting *me*? I am the more formidable soldier. It is my duty and honor to protect *you*."

Lark meets me toe-to-toe, grips my ribs, and pulls me forward to press her lips to mine. "If their weapons are spelled or treated to take you and your brothers off the board, odds are they're going to try to shoot you. My feathers are bulletproof. I can disarm them and keep you from harm."

Before I have time to argue, Mac lets off a throaty curse in the living room. "Are ye havin' a feckin' party back there? What's keepin' ye?"

The sound catapults us both into action and we jostle up the hall, each of us determined to protect the other.

"They've overridden the elevator controls," Lukas shouts, rushing back from the interface console at the elevator. "It seems encountering Link and the others on four slowed them down, but that's over. Company is coming."

"I don't suppose we can say we're not decent to receive guests," Mac says.

Lukas positions himself behind the barrier of the upended table. "I don't suppose, no."

Lark and I race out to join them and Mac gestures to the hand weights. "Flash, yer the only one who can use those as weapons effectively, so have at it."

I glance down at what I brought back from the workout room and assess my options, searching for the greatest probability of success.

Lark positions herself behind the sofa that is now propped on its end and hooked around the corner by the kitchen. It offers us another place to gain cover.

"Flash, whatever yer calculatin', ye need to snap out of it." Mac says, the growl of his Sith cat rumbling behind his words.

"Shift says their ammunition is treated with the takedown serum and can be used against them."

"Good to know, lad, but it'll do ye no good if yer standing in their line of fire when those doors open. We'll work on survivin' and seize our chance when and if the opportunity arises, but how about ye take cover like the rest of us?"

Connor Mac means well, but his defense strategy is flawed in this case. With a greater force in number and strength, allowing the opposing force access into our territory without opposition reduces survivability by twenty-eight percent.

Direct conflict and a surprise ambush are the most probable way to succeed.

Instead of crouching behind their bunker barricade as requested, I grip a twenty-pound hand weight in each hand and launch off the floor. With a few mighty pumps of my wings, I fly straight at the elevator doors, hands extended.

Mac

"FLASH, NO!" The moment Flash launches at the elevator, Lark exposes her position, racing to join him in a flare of ebony feathers. Her wings aren't the massive, eight-foot-long affair like the males of her species, but they're no less powerful—or stunning.

Lukas curses and moves to stand. "They're going to get themselves killed. Does nobody know how to soldier here?"

I feel his pain.

The tinny *bing* announcing the elevator is the only warning we get before those steel doors whisper open and two Gen-3 soldiers come out and snag Flash right out of the fucking air.

Lukas mutters something about being punished by the gods and starts casting magic like the badass mage he is. Spikey balls of blue energy build in his palms and he fires them across the room in quick succession.

I rise, stripping off my clothes as I toe my boots off my feet. "Stay out of the melee as long as ye can. They'll snap ye like a twig if ye get too close."

"Fuck you," Lukas snaps.

I chuckle. "Yeah, I thought ye'd say that."

With that settled, I set my Sith side free. I hate the transition, but my cat is better suited for this fight... and while these soldiers may be conditioned to fight against faery and Elbirfae, they won't be expecting me.

My cat explodes to the fore with an ease I find unsettling. Something has changed since encountering Shift. Well, something other than the constant hard-on I've been sporting day and night.

My transition to my cat comes much faster and hurts less. I'm not sure what that means, but I also don't want to look too closely at it.

My cat explodes into action, crossing the living room and closing the distance to the soldiers exiting into our home away from home.

One of them notices me, but before he can do anything beyond raising his hands to defend, I'm on him. My claws are like knives as I rake through his clothing, slicing through the fabric. Still, I have no effect on his reinforced skin.

Lark groans to my left, locked in a hand-to-hand battle and getting knocked around like a fucking rag doll. The bastard soldier unleashing a flurry of fists and feet upon her sends her reeling across our little arena. I rush forward with a feral roar, leaping onto his back and wrapping my paws around his neck.

I may not understand this bond that's building between Lark, the three, and myself, but my cat doesn't need to understand. My beast is all instinct, and that instinct tells us that Lark is our female.

Ours to protect and teach and one day... maybe more than that.

To batter her is to bring down our wrath.

The super soldier wrestles against the piercing hold of my claws, but I refuse to let go. Elbows clip my ribs with bruising force, and chunks of fur are ripped from my shoulders. No matter how much damage he inflicts on me, I'll never stop fighting.

We roll across the carpeted floor as one.

Grunts and growls mix as I hang on and fight to weaken him. He's definitely stronger... has more stamina... and is more durable... but beyond holding on for the ride, I don't know what else to do.

Another raider advances. He's a satyr by the look of the twigs and sprigs sprouting out of his shoulders. He's got a short sword raised, his sights solidly locked on an otherwise occupied Flash.

I growl, launching off the one I'm fighting to keep that damnable monstrosity of a man from taking down one of my own.

With a fierce roar, I close my mouth around his wrist and whip my head back and forth like a feral cat. The muscles of my jaw, neck, and shoulders remain rigid as my teeth dig harder at the steel of his flesh.

Saliva floods my mouth as I pull harder and harder. Come on, ye fucker....

And then it happens...

A growl of victory rumbles out of my chest as the metallic

taste of blood pools against the back of my tongue. I swallow it down and it feeds something violent and sadistic in me. And now we know these fuckers aren't totally indestructible.

The good news is, there are only two of them.

If that can be considered good news.

The three of us continue to fight, but despite our efforts, Lark and I are getting our asses handed to us no matter how hard we punch, kick, or slice.

I take a few hits myself, but they do nothing more than knock the wind out of me. They're getting more aggressive, and I know that if we don't come up with something fast, one of us is bound to get seriously hurt.

Flash beats back our opponents as Lark and I do our best to stay in the game. Between the three of us, we create a crisscross of attacks while Lukas moves in and tries firing his Glock at them.

Not that it does any good.

His bullets either bounce off them or, if it's a dead-on shot, embed into their skin and then fall to the floor with a metallic *tink.*

There's no way for us to beat indestructible foes.

The only way to survive this is to get the fuck gone. With that in mind, I rush over to where Lukas has dug in behind the dining table and I reclaim my form.

"They're wearing us down." I grab my pants off the floor and pull them on. "The battle has drawn them far enough from the elevator that there's a chance we can get in and get out of this fucking bunker."

Lukas frowns at me. "What's the play?"

I stomp my bare feet into my boots and grab the fire extinguisher off the mounting plate on the kitchen wall. "You try to shoot holes in them and I'll try to put out this fire."

Lukas is already on the move. Jogging forward with his gun raised, he races through the surrounding carnage—broken furniture, demolished walls, and best of all... the bloodstained floors.

Yeah, baby. That was me.

The two of us close the distance to the elevator, navigating the battling bodies. Despite not liking the idea of modified soldiers, I will be the first to admit that Flash is one hell of a fighter with wicked sharp battle skills.

And the same goes for his brothers.

I've been trying to ignore the heavy rock twisting in the pit of my belly. I don't like Shift being upstairs taking on the full squad of these beasts.

Yes, I realize he is a kick-ass soldier, but...

I growl at myself, push down my feelings, and focus on my battle for survival. Still, I send the other team some positive vibes, hoping they are holding their own.

It takes a bit for Lukas and me to get through the chaos of the battle—Flash is facing off with both soldiers and Lark is doing her best to help when and where she can—but eventually, we do.

"Time to go, kids," I say when we're in position.

Flash has a death grip on one of the soldier's arms where my cat gnawed it raw. Yeah, I got that unraveling started. You're welcome.

I hold up the orange canister and get ready for the grand finale. "Lark, Flash, to the elevator. Move."

It seems to take a moment for my words to filter through the adrenaline pumping through their mind and muscles. But the moment I grab Lark's wing and pull her into the elevator car, Flash follows as if tethered to her somehow.

Lark is battered and her footing is sloppy. When I let her go, she stumbles to the back of the massive elevator and slides to the floor.

Lukas fires off a few more rounds and then I release the

nozzle of the extinguisher, sending huge streams of white smoke and powder at them as he thumbs the door close button.

The moment the elevator moves, I take my first deep breath since this all began.

Flash reaches to punch the button panel. "We must stop on four and see—"

I hold out my hand to stop him. "We can't. I'm sorry. We barely escaped with four of us against two. We're not opening the door to face more. For now, we retreat and regroup."

"But my brothers—"

"Your brothers are in a battle and have a weapon that takes down the Gen-3 soldiers. Your strength is needed here. Your duty is to secure Princess Honor's mate and your female."

That seems to settle him quickly enough. He purses his lips and dips his chin. "Understood."

Good. I ignore the glare I'm getting from Lukas and flash him a middle-finger salute. Sure, he outranks me in the field and is one hell of a soldier, but that's when comparing apples to apples.

Those Gen-3 models aren't apples—they're coconuts. Bigger, tougher, and harder to crack. Because with that hard outer shell of theirs, hitting them is pretty much ineffective.

"Flash, tell yer brothers we're headed out of the bunker and to the burned barn. They are to evacuate at their earliest convenience and join us."

Flash nods and his expression blanks out with that far-away look he gets when he's talking cranium to cranium with his brothers.

"Top floor," Lukas says, raising his gun. "Fresh air, freedom, and Gen-3 sweeper soldiers watching the escape exits. On your toes, everyone. Lock it down and get ready for round two."

I sigh. "I was hopin' the two we fought were the guards left up top... since they didn't arrive with the rest of their squad."

"Or the two that dropped off on the second floor to search and who were catching up with the primary group," Lukas adds.

I grunt. "I like my scenario better."

"No doubt."

"Can ye cast an invisibility spell over us or somethin' so we can avoid another skirmish?"

"In the five seconds we have until we're topside? Sorry. I'm good, but I'm not a fucking magician."

I snort and draw my sidearm. "Says the fuckin' magician."

The four of us watch the numbers count off as we rise and I hold a hand out to Lark. "On yer feet, lass. We're not out of the thick of things yet."

Flash and I help her up and though she does well not to complain, there's no missing the injuries she's suffered or the toll they've taken.

When she's on her feet, I pat her arm and offer her a smile. "It's not long now. Home stretch."

"It's fine. I'm tougher than I seem," she says.

"Aye, ye've proven that."

The elevator bumps to a stop and my cat crouches within me, ready to pounce. "Safe home, everyone."

The doors slide apart and my mouth drops open at the fighting force before us. "Holy shit."

CHAPTER FOUR

Shift

a battle can be won or lost in minutes or hours. Not that I know this firsthand because other than the training regimen we performed twelve years ago during our warrior assessments, and the brief skirmish we had with Lark and Connor Mac during our first contact, this is my first true battle.

Still, I imagine the extensive programming and data files embedded in my system feel much the same as genuine experience.

At least I presume it does.

Watching Dune and Tundra battle is impressive.

They are formidable warriors.

When the elevator opened and the attacks began, it was obvious the Amberloq Biome Generals were the most vulnerable. Link and I might be second generation, and Alpha and Beta first generation, but at the core of things, we are genetically enhanced soldiers, the same as the third generation models.

And while Amberloq warriors are the leaders in battle and

protection of the quadrant, in this room, they are at a disadvantage.

But what Dune and Tundra lack in strength and genetic enhancement, they possess in experience, pride, and determination. Even watching them spin through the battlegrounds striking out with their wings, meeting force with force, and taking the blows that would ground an ordinary man, I can't help but be impressed.

Link has always held our status above those they designed us to fight with, but I would be proud to serve alongside an army of Amberloq warriors.

If I ever get the chance.

The neuro-link I share with my brothers opens, and Flash's presence fills my mind. *The two soldiers from the elevator attacked us on the fourth floor, my brothers. We bested them for the moment and are evacuating the bunker. We shall regroup at the burned barn where their fellow soldiers were lost.*

The mention of the burned barn brings back erotic images of Connor Mac claiming my body in the forest outside. *How does my male fare? Is he well?*

His feline fought with a ferocity to be proud of. He is well and whole.

I exhale a breath of relief and thrust a forward kick into my opponent's thigh.

And our catalyst, Lady Lark? Link asks.

She fought at my side and was a fearsome female. She suffered injuries, but none of them seem critical. Her well-being must be assessed when we reunite.

Of course. I will ensure she is well. We have yet to fully understand what her status as our catalyst means.

I will ensure she is well, but not because she is our catalyst. I will watch over her because she is my female.

Thankfully, Flash isn't in the room to see Link's reaction to his claiming of Lark. Either he doesn't understand, or he refuses to acknowledge the pull that is growing between us, Connor, and Lark.

Although Link portrays himself as the strongest and bravest of our three, he is also the most rigid and closed off about the possibility we might someday find our place among the people of the quadrant.

I believe he finds it easier to trust things when it is us against them.

"The other group has evacuated the bunker," I tell Dune as the two of us beat back a burly male with short shaved hair. "We are to evacuate at our earliest convenience and join them."

Dune pikes backward, avoiding a roundhouse kick to his side, and grunts. "We'll get right on that. It's too bad you let them destroy the gun before we could take them all down. That would've been so much more convenient."

I lift my arm and block an overhead strike from a lanky tattooed male. "I didn't *let* them destroy it. The moment I began using it against them, they opted to destroy them rather than us use them. At least that left us on even footing."

Dune grunts. "Yeah, *even*."

I continue to take on my opponent, and while my comment isn't totally accurate, it's not far off. We took four down with the serum shots left us with six against six. The only true inequality is the fact that Dune and Tundra don't have heightened genetics.

They are not powerless in the battle, but they seem to tire after taking and giving a barrage of constant blows.

Link is facing the greatest threat. The foe he battles is a great leonine beast trying to fell his prey in a battle of claws and ferocity. With his long flowing mane of ebony hair framing his black face, a wide-brimmed nose, and his vertically slit golden eyes, he can be nothing other than a member of the feline folk.

And by his size, he is an alpha of his kind.

The two have been going at one another for too long for our

foes not to realize they overestimated whatever advantage they thought they possessed going into this battle.

We are neither defective nor inferior.

The chime of the elevator arriving at our floor rings out and all heads turn to gauge the incoming forces.

"Hells, yes!" Dune shouts, raising a fist into the air. "What the slecking hell took you so long, boys? It's not like we're on a picnic here."

A flood of military men hemorrhages onto the floor and the odds shift heavily in our favor. Even without them being genetically altered soldiers, Connor Mac's military forces have the tactical training and sheer numbers to ensure our victory.

The Gen-3 soldiers seem to come to the same conclusion because, with the rise of a clawed fist and a mighty roar of fury, the lion man changes the dynamic of the fight.

The immediate shift of focus from Brass's army has us all turning toward the elevator and the incoming human force arriving as our backup.

"Blow it," the lion man growls.

Before I wonder what he's ordering to be blown, an explosion sounds off somewhere far above us and then the Gen-3 soldiers are barreling through the human enforcers.

An incredible crashing sound follows the explosion and the floor shakes.

"Do they intend to bury us down here?" Dune asks, scowling at our surroundings.

The ear-splitting shriek of metal scraping down the inside of the elevator shaft has me turning down my auditory sensors. It's sharp and piercing, and worse than that, it seems never-ending.

Being four floors below ground, it takes time for the debris to fall past our floor and then the shriek continues in the shaft below us.

The lion man and one of his soldiers—a dragon shifter, judging by his size and strength—yank the elevator doors from the housings and glance down the shaft at the falling debris and rubble.

Opening those doors makes the noise of the destruction so much worse.

"Move!" the lion bellows.

One-by-one, the six opposing fighters withdraw from the fight, engage their wings, and take a running leap to launch skyward into the dark shaft.

I move to follow, but Tundra grabs my wrist. "Let them go. We have the advantage here and now, but if they lead us into the clutch of the others of their kind, we will be outnumbered and spent from the battle already fought. For now, we will celebrate our win."

"Our win?" Link repeats, his face screwed up in a scowl. "I fail to see our victory."

Tundra sits on the side of an upturned desk and wipes his brow. "Well, we came out of the battle with no loss of life, Flash took down two of their army for us to question and examine, and somewhere around here, there are guns with serum-tainted bullets we can give to our scientists."

Dune grins, tugging the tattered rags of his shirt off his chest and wiping his face and arms with them. "That's a solid win, boys. Think about it. Before this battle, we didn't know what we were dealing with and nowhere to begin in figuring it out."

I stretch out my arms and roll my shoulders, my heart still pumping blood and adrenaline at a powerful rate. "I understand your logic, but that's not how our programming views a victory."

Tundra offers me an extended hand and I help him back to his feet. "You're an Amberloq now, my friend. Adapt your programming to real-world examples instead of what a bunch of scientists decided. Take the win."

Taking his advice, I jog over to where I last saw the gun

when I was disarmed and search the rubble of what was once an administrative area of this facility.

After shoving a couple of desk chairs out of the way and sifting through the contents of a downed bookshelf, I find the broken weapon.

The magazine is cracked, and the bullets within it are exposed. I lift it, paying careful attention not to touch the ammunition. "Would one of you gentlemen like to take possession of this, please?"

Dune jogs over and accepts my offering with a wink and a smile. "See. A win."

I have my own idea of what a celebration of winning looks like. It's framed by russet red hair, hazel eyes, and a heated look I know angers him, but he doesn't can't fight.

And I can't get any of that down here.

Without another word, I jog to the empty cavity where the elevator used to be and I fly up five flights and into the night sky.

Straight into the night sky.

The generation three soldiers blew the top of the elevator shaft away and, in the process, the mechanics, the top of the shaft, and the warehouse ceiling.

It was a dramatic yet effective way to create an alternate escape route.

Shooting straight up and into the cool, fresh air of the night, I reposition my wings and arc my back to take me to the crowd of soldiers gathering by the trucks below.

Normally, my attention would be drawn to my brother Flash, but it isn't him my senses seek and find.

Landing beside my male, I fold my wings and study him with both my eyes and my diagnostic sensors. "Are you well?"

I scan the body I have become so hearteningly aware of over the past week. He looks strong, handsome, and fit. I yearn to embrace him, or at the very least touch his bare arm, but remind myself he does not welcome signs of affection in front of his men.

He made that very clear during our first outing at the burned-out barn.

When he lets off a low chuckle, I catch the arch of his brow. "Are ye finished yer inventory?"

I feel the warmth of a blush heat my cheeks. "Forgive me. My concern for your safety temporarily distracted me from your need for discretion."

He puts me out of my misery by giving me the connection I seek and squeezing my upper arm. "It's fine. And I'm fine. Ye needn't look so concerned. All is well."

Yes, it seems it is. I extend my assessment beyond Mac to meet the concerned gaze of Flash and the unfocused gaze of our female. "Lady Lark, are you well?"

"No. I don't think she is," Flash says aloud. Then our private communication channel opens, and he speaks directly into my mind. *She fought with fire and determination beyond her skills and her strength. In doing so, she suffered many devastating blows. I fear something is wrong, and she is either too stubborn or too stunned to realize she is unwell.*

I will assess her and —

Lark gives us a little wave and a deep frown. When she turns to face us, her ebony feathers ruffle as her wings flex. "I'm fine, boys. Please don't talk about me behind my back."

"Apologies, Lady Lark. We simply—"

She stiffens and holds up both hands, closing her eyes. "And *pleeease* stop with the Lady Lark. I'm just Lark. If I'm your catalyst and we're bound for whatever that means from now on, I don't want to be fawned over."

Flash frowns and takes one of her hands in his. "Apologies. We have never had anyone to care about before, or had anyone who cared about us. If we are handling it wrong, I swear we will do better."

She closes her eyes and exhales. After a few deep breaths, she seems to have reset her settings somewhat, for when she opens her eyes, the warmth we are becoming accustomed to has returned. "It's me who should apologize. You're right, this is all new to you and you've done nothing wrong. I'm just tired, and a little banged up from the battle. Forgive me for being short with you."

Flash slides in closer and kisses her cheek. "You need never ask us for forgiveness, my lovely. You are our catalyst and, as such, are our most precious gift."

I squeeze her hand and kiss her other cheek. "Flash is correct. We owe you everything. We only want your health and happiness in return."

"Is there a problem?" Link asks as he joins our conversation. He arrives with Alpha and Beta at his side. "Are you well, Lady Lark? You look…"

I hold up my hand. "She does not wish to be called Lady Lark any longer. She is just Lark."

Link shrugs. "Just Lark it is then."

Mac chuckles beside me and I shift my attention to him. "What do you find amusing?"

He clears his throat and meets Lark's gaze. "I think ye misunderstood when she said 'just Lark'. She simply meant to be called Lark."

Lark rolls her eyes. "Yes, that's it. I want my name only. Lark. I am Lark."

I nod. "That makes more sense."

Mac seems to find this entire exchange amusing. The man has a lovely smile, and I can see by the crinkles beside his eyes that he enjoys laughing. It is a very attractive look for him.

"Greetings, Lark. It is an honor," Alpha says, offering her his open palm. "I am the genetic prototype Alpha-6 and this is Beta-4."

Lark shakes each of their hands. "The pleasure is mine.

Thank you for helping us survive down there. I'm sorry we didn't wake you sooner."

Alpha shrugs. "To serve the crown and the quadrant of Dornte is our purpose and honor. Whether that began now or two days ago is irrelevant next to the decades we have lain in stasis."

Lark's frown deepens. "I am so sorry you both were judged and left in those cylinders for so many years. I promise we will do better than those who came before us."

Alpha looks at me and smiles. "You are correct. Your catalyst is lovely."

It's funny. His comment is nothing but a restatement of truth, but I feel a little shy and uncertain when I meet Lark's gaze. "Yes. She is."

Lukas finishes speaking to his men and then joins us. "Are you folks ready to get out of here?"

Mac checks with each of us and then answers for the group. "Sounds good. Where to?"

"Honor wanted you back with us at Amberloq Hall, but I still don't like it. If Brass sent his army to eliminate you, I don't want to draw the next attempt to Thornebane Castle. There are too many innocents."

"Then where?"

Dune grins and lays a heavy hand across my shoulders. "You're moving up in the world, boys. We're taking you to the Amberloq retreat on Mount Nekko. We were headed there to get ready for the warrior trials, so looks like we'll be roomies."

Flash grins. "You're not putting us back in stasis?"

Lukas shakes his head. "No. Your days of being trapped in your own minds are over. Keep doing what you're doing and show us you truly are an asset to the Guardians of the Crown and you'll be free to live the life they created you for."

The news is as shocking as it is unexpected.

Flash looks like he might overload his systems as he picks up

Lark and swings her in a circle in his arms as he kisses her. "You made this possible, my lovely. How will we ever thank you?"

Lark looks a little green and pats his shoulder. "Putting me down would be a start."

Mac's hazel eyes are alight with joy and I want to embrace him and kiss him as Flash did with Lark, but with the eyes of his fellow soldiers upon us, I know he wouldn't welcome it.

Instead, I hug Lark and kiss her forehead. "Thank you. There is no way you can truly understand how you changed the outcome of our existence. We will forever be your humble soldiers."

Lark eases back, looking unsettled. "If we have a journey ahead of us, we should go."

CHAPTER FIVE

Mac

"That boy's got it bad for you, Mac. He's in full starry-eyed lurve with you." Lukas' tone holds too much amusement.

I fight the urge to tackle him out of the pilot's seat and pound him against the helicopter floor. Thankfully, I have a bit more self-preservation than that.

Instead, I adjust the headset, angle the mic, and glance out the helicopter's side window, trying to figure out what kind of answer I'm supposed to give him. Anyone with eyes can see there's something happening between Shift and me.

Even without the PDA he so desperately craves, there's the tension between us while we're trying *not* to look at or touch one another.

"Hey, I'm just fucking with you, man. You and I go way back. I've seen your crash-and-burn moments and you've seen mine. You don't need to front. Tell me… what's up?"

I swallow and allow my gaze to swing to where Shift is flying with his brothers, Lark, Dune, and Tundra. Damn, he really is sexy AF. Wearing only worn jeans and hiking boots, there's very little blocking my view of all that golden skin. The guy is ripped like they chiseled him from granite. And then there are his wings.

Unlike the beautiful feathers of the Elbirfae, the wings of the enhanced soldiers are more like hard plates that can be used as a metal shield or blades at the ends.

And as I watch his golden skin and that soft as silk blond hair of his gracefully cut through the violet sky, I can't deny my chest is tight, my cock is hard, and my cat is prowling. "It's not natural. The way I want him... I just feel like I'm bein' manipulated."

"By Shift?"

"Och, no. They were designed as spies, but neither he nor Flash has an ounce of guile with their affections. It's damned annoyin' actually."

Lukas chuckles. "Shadow is a lot like that. And yeah, at first it was embarrassing and frustrating to know that people knew my business and I wasn't coming off as the elusive, macho stud everyone thought I was."

I snort. "No one thought that."

"Well, okay, maybe it was only me who thought that, but yeah, it's unsettling for men like us to have our personal shit right out there."

"But what is my personal shit? Four days ago, I was geared up to take down a science experiment I found utterly offensive. Now I'm runnin' a litany of tapes in my head, tellin' myself that I don't really feel a pull to the male. That I don't want him pinned beneath me. That I don't want—"

"—Yep, I get it."

I sigh. "So, what happens when we're secluded on the peak of a mountain?"

"Hey, I'm the last person to give advice on how to lock your emotions down and deny that kind of pull. I did such a shit job hiding my need for Shadow, that Honor not only saw it, she encouraged me to get out of my own way and acknowledge it."

"She's one hell of a female."

Staring out at the night sky beyond the helicopter, his face breaks out in a totally sappy smile. "Yeah, she is. So, I know what you're saying. With all the hours I spent breaking her free from that fucking spell, I wanted her and had fallen for her before she even woke from her coma. There was no helping it."

I rub my palms against my thighs and growl. "But the three of them are tied to Lark too. It's a shit show. I can see things with Lark, but I don't feel the same pull fer Flash... and Link is one arrogant fucker."

He laughs. "Arrogant. Have you met Dune? Do you think I wanted to cozy up to him in the beginning? Fuck, we came to blows more than once."

I let my head drop back and run my fingers through my hair. "It's so damned messy."

"Yep. But sometimes messy is fun."

I flash him a droll stare and shake my head. "And where the hell will the other two fit in?"

"Alpha and Beta?"

"Yeah. That's too many fucking cocks in one relationship."

Lukas busts up laughing. "I don't think you have to worry about that. Alpha and Beta were designed before Brass aimed for full integration. They don't have genitalia."

My mouth drops open. "Are ye serious? The bastard didn't even give them the decency of a complete mold?"

"Nope. I guess you're lucky that Shift and his brothers were the next iterations and got the goods."

I don't even know what to say about that. Glancing out the helicopter window, I take in the newest members of the bio-engineered soldiers.

Alpha and Beta are both large-stature, rugged males built very much to look like fae. They have elongated ears like an elf, but their wings don't seem to be retractable like Shift and his brothers'.

Alpha has heavy, green, rounded wings much like the Elbir-fae, but Beta's wings are delicate, much more faery-like. They blaze in shades of gold, orange, and crimson and are trimmed with black edges that look wicked sharp.

"Do ye think it'll be a case of them not havin' sexual impulses or them sufferin' because they don't have the equipment?"

Lukas casts a sideways glance at me and shrugs. "I honestly didn't give another male's junk that much thought."

Okay, I see his point. Maybe I'm projecting.

Watching the five engineered soldiers doesn't help the turmoil of my mind a damn bit. I went from hating everything they represent to being fully empathetic to them, what's been done to them, and what that will mean in the future.

Then I look at Lark. The way she flies alongside them, at ease with them after only a few days. She is to Flash what I think I am to Shift and yet she doesn't try to shut him down. She's not afraid of admitting there's something powerful and magical at play here.

She's braver than me.

I'm still studying her when I notice her shake her head. Her body is sleek, and normally the grace of her flight could make a male swoon, but something is off. "The lass is strugglin'."

"What do you mean?" Lukas asks, sitting higher in his seat to get a look past Dune and Tundra. "Struggling how?"

I seem to be the only one looking at her when her head falls forward and then her wings fall limp. In one heartbeat, she drops out of formation and plummets toward the ground.

"She's going down!"

Flash

THE MOMENT LARK falls still and drops from our flock, I swear my heart stops despite what a system scan would show. Her body is motionless, her ebony hair flowing behind her as the jagged peaks of mountains below spear ever closer. The moment I collect her into my arms, I know it's bad. Her entire frame is limp.

What happened? Shift asks, quickly dropping to fly at my side.

I don't know. Despite what she said, she didn't fare well in that battle. She took too many hits trying to fight at my side.

Internal bleeding? Link asks, joining us.

I expect so, yes, Shift says. *Although I won't know for sure until I can examine her.*

I scan the hostile mountain landscape below. *There's nowhere we can land and make her comfortable.*

And it's been twenty minutes since we passed the last settlement at the foothills of the mountains, Shift adds.

"How far is this retreat of yours?" Link asks Dune. "Lady Lark needs medical attention and Shift cannot heal her here."

"We're almost there," Dune says. "Five minutes if we push."

I nod, pulling her more securely into my arms. "Then we push."

The flight is a blur and though my programming ensures, I can filter through stress, Andras Brass must have overlooked the emotional stabilization needed during a romantic entanglement. Because regardless of my cognitive functions, I am losing my mind by the time Dune points down toward a massive compound built into the side of a mountain.

"Hang on, my lovely. We are here now. Shift will fix you in just a few minutes. Stay with us."

The next few minutes are—again—a blur.

"Hold your elevation while I disarm the security protocols," Tundra says.

I watch as the white of his wings blends in with the snow-capped peaks below and the delay is almost too much to bear.

"Just a few more minutes and you'll be out of the cold and Shift will take care of you." I kiss her temple and my heart shudders in my chest. "Her skin feels so sticky against my lips."

Shift is watching her with honed focus and I know he has already begun his initial scans. "Her pulse is racing and her core temperature is running hot."

"Then let's get her looked at," Dune says, gesturing to where Tundra is waving us down to the compound. We land in an expansive outdoor training area and are ushered inside the ten-foot-tall blood red doors while the helicopter lands behind us.

And then we're running.

"The medical bay is through here," Dune says, leading the way.

It seems surreal, us running to the medical bay at the Amberloq mountain retreat. After more than a decade of nothing happening and us wishing for adventure and battle... how has this become our lives?

"Lay her on the table, my brother," Shift says, rushing over to wash his hands. "And remove her clothing so I can examine her."

Tundra pulls a supply cart out of the cupboard and closes the distance between us. The sight of the vacuum-sealed surgical equipment turns my stomach.

To avoid a full ejection of my insides, I grab the strange scissors and cut along the center of Lark's top. "Anyone who doesn't need to be here, leave. Lark deserves her modesty."

Link steps to the side, and with his back against the wall, he crosses his arms. Alpha and Beta leave with Dune and Tundra, but the departures end there.

Lukas squeezes my shoulder and comes to stand at the table. "Mac has field training. I have magical gifts. And your boy, Shift, is the man with magical molecular healing. Between the three of us, she's in excellent hands."

I read the dilation ratio of his pupils and determine he is

worried but genuine. He truly believes between the three of them, Lark will be all right.

When I move to cut off her leather pants, Mac stays my hand. "How about we undo them and take them off so she has somethin' to wear when she's well?"

I check with Shift and he nods. "It's fine. Lukas and I can stabilize her upper body. It might even be faster than trying to cut the reinforced leather."

In the end, Connor Mac is right and peeling Lark's pants down her thighs is the work of a moment. Taking her boots off beforehand would've been a good idea, but hindsight and all that.

"She looks so pale." I hate the lack of color in her cheeks. To compliment her ebony hair and deep green eyes, Lark normally carries the healthy, tanned complexion of the people of her Forested Jungle Biome.

Tonight, she's as pale as Tundra's wings.

I watch Lukas' hands glow and Shift's hands smooth over her bruised flesh and I hate the evidence of her injuries. We knew her training was lacking, and she wasn't ready for much of a battle, and yet it never slowed her down in the slightest.

Lark may be all feminine curves and beauty, but beneath the soft lines and velvet skin, there beats the heart of a warrior.

When I replay the images of the battle in my mind, I'm both proud and horrified. "Never once did she shy away from a hit or fall back to save herself the beating. I tried to keep them off her, but—"

"Och, don't do that, lad," Mac says, moving in front of me. "Ye care fer her—we all see it—and because ye do, ye did yer best to keep her safe. Don't blame yerself fer this. Whatever her injuries are, they didn't come by yer actions, and Lukas and Shift will fix them right up, won't ye boys?"

Lukas is running his hold down Lark's thighs, his palms

glowing with a magical energy that lifts the hair on my arms. "You know it."

I look to Shift for him to confirm what Lukas says is true... but he isn't looking up at me. "Brother? Will she be well?"

Shift frowns. "She has several contusions to the head, three badly bruised ribs, and a small bleed at the base of her skull. I am running a full scan of her system now to ensure there are no other areas of injury."

"But will she be well?"

"It is too soon to offer an outcome. Ask me later."

It feels like his words cleave me in two.

I wanted him to say he expects she'll be bruised and sore when she wakes, but that she is in no immediate danger. I press a hand to the tightness in my chest. "It feels like I've been trapped under a great weight and the pressure is crushing me."

"Breathe, lad," Mac says, cupping my jaw in his palms. "Ye look like ye might be the next one to collapse. Let's keep it to one patient at a time, aye? Focus on my eyes and take a few deep breaths."

I don't like not being able to see Lark, but the room feels hotter than the temperature suggests. "My equilibrium regulator seems to be malfunctioning."

Mac's gaze softens. "I'm not surprised yer dizzy. Yer wound tighter than a top. Now do as I say and—"

The wall behind my back seems to give way and my feet slide out from under me.

"—aye, yep, here we go." Mac grips under my arms and then Link is grabbing my elbow and bending to help me to the ground. When my backside is firmly planted on the ground, I blink and find myself falling into Mac's rich hazel eyes. "There now. How about ye try again and breathe, aye?"

"What's wrong with me?" I initiate a self-diagnostic. "All my systems are functioning, but my chest is constricted and my ocular assessment is skewed. Am I defective?"

Mac is kneeling before me and he chuckles. "Yer in love, lad. And when the object of our affection is hurt and in danger of dyin', it's enough to floor the mightiest of warriors. Trust me, yer not alone and yer certainly not defective."

Dune comes through the doorway to our right and cants his head to the side. "What did I miss?"

"Nothin' worth repeatin'," Mac says. "Can we get a bedroom ready where Lark can rest? And if possible, make the bed big enough fer Flash to lie with her. I have a feelin' our boy here will need a little quiet time reassurin' himself his female is all right."

Dune chuckles and points a thumb over his shoulder. "Our training retreat is your training retreat. Let me know when you're ready to move and I'll get you set up. Oh, and Tundra's got a midnight meal cooking on the grill for those who need to refuel."

CHAPTER SIX

Lark

$\mathcal{J}$ wake to an erotic tingling in my core, and gentle hands caressing my collarbone and shoulders. The sensation is wholly out of place because the last thing I remember is the battle in the bunker and feeling like I'd been run over by a public conveyance.

This is an enormous improvement.

In fact, it's such an enormous improvement I almost don't want to wake from what is obviously a dream... a super sexy dream.

And what's with my sex drive weighing in every ten minutes? I spent two years living in crowded barracks in that goblin compound and other than a few desperate moments to take the edge off and remind myself I was a woman with needs; I was content.

Now my body seems focused on orgasms.

Wanting them. Having them. Sharing them.

I stretch, and the friction of soft sheets against my bare legs and belly tells me I'm not wearing any clothes. The friction only adds to my state of longing, and I groan.

Seriously, what is going on with me?

My eyes are still so heavy I'm not sure I even want to open them and ruin this moment. All I know is I am naked and for the first time in as long as I can remember, I'm relaxed and feeling pampered and sexy.

"You are so beautiful." The smooth timbre of Shift's voice warms me from the inside out. "Hear the truth in my words, Lark. You are safe and well and in expert hands. Relax and let me finish your healing."

The magic of his touch is massaging the aches and injuries out of my body, replacing the negative with the most sensual positives I think I've ever experienced. Has any man ever massaged me like this?

No. Never.

And though his hands are on my shoulders, kneading the tension of battle from my arms, I feel his touch in an entirely different part of my body. My core is damp and throbbing, aching for a little of his healing touch.

I scissor my legs under the sheets, hungry for more than friction.

Whatever was wrong with me after the battle has been thoroughly taken care of because I feel more alive than ever before.

I swallow and let myself sink deeper into the bliss of his touch. "Your hands are incredible. You've got a genuine gift."

The deep-throated chuckle close to my ear awakens even more of my feminine desire. "It is the gift *you* awoke in me, beautiful. It is only fitting you should enjoy the results."

His words are whispered close to my ear in soft reference, his breath a warm caress against my neck. The sensation tickles my skin and my nipples tighten.

"Do all your patients wake this wanton?" I ask, absently, my eyes still closed because I don't want to break the spell. "That might get awkward."

He chuckles quietly above my head. "No. When I touch you, the connection we have is something unique and sensual. I believe it's because of our bond. You are ours, as we are yours. There is magic at work."

There definitely is.

The thought of that connection brings my need to a higher level. I groan, shifting my legs beneath the sheets as warmth pools at my core. "And how far does your dedication to patient care extend?"

He chuckles again. "You are a very special patient and I am a very dedicated healer. What is it you need?"

"Everything. All of you."

Opening my eyes, I realize my fear of breaking this spell is irrelevant. The golden glow of a hundred tiny candles spread around the room, washes the bedroom with a magical feel. It amplifies my impression that something otherworldly is happening.

I meet Shift's honey-gold gaze and exhale a sigh. "I take it you saved me from something I suffered during the battle?"

His crooked smile is too sexy. "It was my deepest pleasure to ensure your recovery, though I can't take all the credit. Lukas was there and kept you stable while I worked. And it was Flash who caught you mid-flight and kept you safe until we arrived here and I could heal you."

I lift my hands, reaching above my head to frame his chiseled jaw. His skin is warm and soft and he's right. Simply touching him washes me with a sense of ownership and belonging.

Is this the way they feel about me?

"I need to kiss you," I say, nipping my bottom lip. "But I don't want to cause issues with Flash or Mac. I'm not exactly sure what we're navigating here."

He lowers his lips to brush against mine. "I foresee no issues.

You are mine as you are Flash's. And as for Connor Mac, well, there have been no claims lain beyond my own. I see no reason you can't have your wish. If a kiss is what you desire, a kiss is what you shall have."

His lips meet mine with a gentle curiosity I find endearing. His kiss is warm, but having him upside down doesn't give me the access I crave.

I swallow. "And if I asked you to undress and join me in this bed, would that cause any issues? Feel free to say no, but I find I've woken with an incredible hunger for your magical touch."

The smile that breaks across his face is nothing short of stunning. "It would honor me to join with you and ease your hunger. Do you truly feel well enough? Your body is recovering from several serious physical injuries. I don't want to cause any discomfort."

The way the deep timbre of his voice vibrates through me is too much. "The only discomfort I'm suffering from is needing you inside of me, but if you're worried, you can go slow and take your time."

His mouth curves with a smile that suggests he likes my gentle tease.

As he steps around to the side of the bed, I get a good look at him and realize he's not wearing a shirt.

I'm not sure what it is about their programing that keeps them from embracing clothing, but I'm not complaining. The three of them were created in the image of physical perfection.

You'd think I'd be getting desensitized by now, but with bodies like theirs, I doubt that will happen.

He leans down to reclaim our kiss and swallows the sound of my sigh of pleasure. Better. Having him face-to-face and being able to move our mouths without the awkwardness of him being upside down is much better.

He slides a hand along my jaw and into my hair at the back of my neck and when he eases back, the grin he gives me brings another flood of moisture to my core. "Kissing you is very nice."

I run a hand down the muscled ridges of his ribs and tug at the button of his cargo pants. "Take these off and climb under the covers with me."

Another blessing of him wearing so little is that him getting naked is the work of a moment. After unfastening his button, he shoves his pants down his muscled thighs and then scissors his feet to free his legs completely.

I grip the edge of the sheet, peeling back the covering to expose my body, which I'm surprised to see isn't as naked as I thought.

Shift takes one look at my bra and panties and his grin grows even wider. "Another gift you bestow upon me. May I undress you?"

"Please do."

Shift's gaze is filled with sheer delight as he draws a finger into the valley of my cleavage and over the clasp of my bra. The awe in his gaze is humbling. The excitement when he studies the mounds of my breasts is adorable.

When he catches me watching him, his cheeks flush. "Apologies. They are so... entrancing."

I take his hand in mine and place his palm so that he's cupping my breast. "Surely, you saw them during the time you've been healing me."

He grows serious and meets my gaze. "While you were vulnerable, none of us took the liberty of looking at you beyond the scope of your healing. Flash cleared the room and demanded your privacy be respected."

The mention of Flash opens a pit of guilt. "Is he all right? He must be so worried."

Maybe this isn't such a good idea.

Shift must sense my concern or see something in my expression because he grows serious. "Why do you withdraw? Have I done something wrong?"

"No. You've been perfect. I just... we haven't talked about expectations and I would never want to hurt him."

"Your happiness could never hurt me, my lovely."

I gasp as Flash's words find me tracing my hand down his naked brother. Searching the shadows, I barely make out the silhouette of a man rising from a seat in the room's corner. "Wait. Have you been here the whole time?"

"Of course. Where else would I be?"

Shift smiles, his touch going back into exploration mode as his attention shifts from my cleavage down my navel to the elastic band of my underwear. "Flash hasn't left your side. You are his, and they hurt you."

"And now you are well." Flash strides forward, running a warm hand up the inside of my bare thigh. "And you are hungry for the pleasure of release."

That's the understatement of the century.

Having them both here, stroking their exploratory touches over my body—it's incredibly erotic. "And that doesn't bother you?"

Flash releases the clasp to my bra and leans in for a kiss at the same time Shift's hand slides under the thin fabric of my underwear. I gasp as his fingers find the seam of my slit, glide through the moisture, and slide inside me.

Flash's eyes are practically glowing in the golden light of the candles. "How could your pleasure bother me? The sounds you make when you are aroused, the way your body arches and quakes... it has become my secondary directive. First, protect the Crown of Dornte. Second, tend to my female."

My back arches as my hips rise to Shift's touch.

I shiver as Flash palms my breast, trapping my nipple between his thumb and forefinger. With his gaze locked on mine, he squeezes, lighting off a sudden burst of painful pleasure.

I moan, caught between needing so much more of this and wanting to make sure I'm not taking advantage of them. I don't want to only teach them the things that benefit me.

That would be selfish.

At this moment, I *really* want to be selfish.

I want nothing more than to accept what they are so obviously willing to give and focus on the moment.

But I can't.

"We need to talk for just a moment, if you don't mind." My voice is weak and breathy. I don't even sound convincing to myself.

Shift withdraws his hand and slides his glistening middle finger into his mouth. His eyes flutter closed, as if the taste of me is something he wants to savor.

I draw a deep breath and fight to hold their gazes instead of getting into all this now. I can't. If this is meant to be, clarifying beforehand shouldn't affect anything. "There are different relationships between lovers. Some are exclusive, just between two people, and some are more inclusive of others. What matters most is that within a relationship, everyone is clear on the expectations."

"Meaning?" Shift asks, his attention wandering as he trails a finger around my nipple and smiling as my nipple buds even tighter.

"Meaning I don't want there to be misgiving between any of us. You three have been a solid unit since your activation. I don't want to cause a strain on that."

Flash grins. "And you worry that us wanting to pleasure you might cause a strain on our bond of brotherhood?"

This conversation has gotten strange. "It concerns me, yes."

Flash straightens and studies Shift, tracing his fingers over the contours of my body. "The only strain I feel is from the restriction of my pants. When I see Shift caress your body, I find his arousal pleasing, for I know the pleasure of being squeezed by your core as you find your height of pleasure. I want both my brothers to experience that, and I want you to feel that, too."

I pull the thin sheet up my body and hug it under my arms while I let that sink in. It's a flimsy shield against the intimacy of that declaration, but it allows me to feel slightly less exposed.

Flash frowns. "Is that wrong?"

"Absolutely not. There's nothing wrong, it's just… well, the expectations in a relationship can be overwhelming and with four of us being bound—"

"—Five of us," Shift corrects. "Connor Mac is mine and we are yours, so there are five of us."

I swallow. "Right. Five in a relationship is bound to get complicated. I want to ensure we are clear on things so everyone's expectations are considered."

Shift and Flash look at one another and then nod.

"You are mine," Flash says. "I enjoy joining with you and wish to do that often."

Shift nods. "And Connor Mac is mine. I also enjoyed joining with him, but I am also yours and want to pleasure you and join with you, as Flash did."

"Oh, boy."

Flash tilts his head. "Do our expectations concern you, my lovely? Should we not wish to pleasure you and Connor Mac and share intimacy?"

Is it hot in here? "Ah, no, that's understandable. Although, I'm not sure Link will feel that way. I don't think he likes or trusts me much."

"Link doesn't like or trust anyone," Shift says, matter-of-factly. "But the experience of joining with you and finding pleasure with one another while including my brothers in a relationship… you find that acceptable?"

Seriously? "Yes, I do."

"And Connor Mac?"

"I can't speak for Mac or guess what kind of relationship he might want. That is a conversation we can't have without him being involved."

Shift seems to consider that. "But you find the idea of the three of us being your lovers acceptable."

Damn, thanks to this conversation, my panties are wet. "I, uh... yes. I feel the pull of whatever is binding us, and I am intrigued to explore the relationship I have with you."

"As lovers," Flash says.

"As lovers and friends," I correct. "I don't just want to have sex. I want to understand why the magic of the universe has paired us together. I want there to be a genuine relationship."

"But we will also have sex," Flash clarifies.

I chuckle. "I hope so, yes."

Shift nods. "I look forward to sharing that kind of intimacy together and think you both would enjoy having Connor Mac thrusting into you. The sensual sting of his penetration was a pleasure I wish to revisit again soon."

As Shift talks about Mac, his cock gets even harder and more glorious.

"Yes, I want that too," Flash says, nodding. "He was kind to me when Lark's injuries overwhelmed me. I find I share an affection for him. I also like the bits of gold and brown that dance in his green eyes."

Shift grins. "Yes, I enjoy those, too. And when he is aroused, the gold expands and nearly blocks out the green. I believe it has something to do with the animal of his Sith side prowling to the fore. It is quite intoxicating."

Oh, my. If anyone had told me a week ago that I would be lying here naked with two mind-blowingly hot guys discussing our five-way bonding, I would've thought them crazy.

"And while the two of you talking about wanting to be taken

by Mac is hot, that's a conversation you should have with him present. In the meantime, I'm interested in what the two of you might want to do with me right now. Flash, would you like to get undressed and join us?"

His grin is full of sinful promise. "I would, very much, but I hear your stomach growling. You are hungry for more than men."

I open my mouth to argue, but at the same moment, my traitorous stomach lets off an embarrassingly aggressive growl.

Shift frowns. "You are right, of course, Flash. Her need for nourishment is more important. Especially after the injuries she sustained."

"No. He's not right." I shake my head. "Trust me. I'm a big girl. My need for threesome sex with the two of you is much greater than my need for food."

Flash chuckles. "You are precious. You speak as if having one excludes the other. It's simply a matter of timing. First, we shall feed you."

Shift nods, bends to give me a glorious view of the dimples cutting the sides of his muscled ass cheeks, and then pulls his pants back on, depriving me of what I want even more than a meal.

Disappointing.

Flash chuckles, brushing his thumb over my lip. "You look so despondent."

Shift catches me ogling him and smiles. "I take it my physical appearance pleases you?"

"Yes, very much. I'm sure your physical appearance will please pretty much everyone you come in contact with."

"Will they all wish to join with me and have sex?"

I frown. "They might *want* to, but that doesn't mean it's going to happen. Remember what I said about the relationship of lovers?"

"I remember everything. It's part of my system design," Shift says. "Are you referring to your comment about being clear about our lovers' expectations?"

"Yes. So, let me be very clear about my expectations if we are to build a relationship."

Both of them straighten, giving me their attention.

"I have no problem being casual if my partner is interested in other lovers, but that's not the sense I get from what's building between us."

Flash shakes his head. "No. You are mine."

"And if I am yours, then while you're in a relationship with me, you are mine as well. It doesn't matter who else finds you attractive or how curious you are about other people—we are a unit."

"You, us, and Connor Mac," Shift says.

I nod. "However, that works, but yes, five of us is quite enough. That means we don't step outside of that relationship for sex. To do that is called cheating or being unfaithful and it's very bad. It will break the trust we're building. Do you understand?"

"You are expressing your expectation of what the relation-ship will mean," Flash says. "The two of us, Connor Mac, and Link only."

"However, that works, yes."

Shift grins. "Understood. Now, can we feed you so we can get naked again and become lovers?"

I chuckle, though there is nothing funny about the wanton ache thrumming in my core. "Yes, please. The sooner the better."

CHAPTER SEVEN

Link

Sitting with Alpha and Beta in the great room of the Mount Nekko mountain lodge, the three of us are lost in what we should do with ourselves. Having never had free time, we find it awkward to know what is expected of us.

"We could explore the building," I suggest, craning my head to take in our surroundings.

"Tundra mentioned an extensive library at the top of the landing on the second floor," Beta says. "Taking in new information is always good."

"I agree, but perhaps having a tactical understanding of the building, its exits, and the perimeter would be good, too."

Alpha nods. "Especially with the threat of attack from the generation three soldiers should they follow us here."

"Do you think they are aware Andras has deviated from the directive of the program?" Beta asks.

I stand, too unsettled to sit for too long. "Does it matter?"

"In the sense that perhaps they are being misled and could be realigned with intervention, yes."

He has a point. "Perhaps Lukas and his team will learn more from the four soldiers we incapacitated."

"And what of us?" Alpha asks. "What should we expect now that the immediate danger has passed?"

I genuinely don't know how to answer that. "At first, when Princess Honor came to the bunker, they intended to decommission the program. When she learned of our time spent suspended in our stasis cylinders, she swore that as long as we didn't betray the crown or try to escape, we will be treated as members of the quadrant."

"Do you believe her?" Alpha asks.

"She has given us no reason not to." I pace around the end of the massive sofa and examine the strange rectangular table sitting there. "What do you suppose they use this table for? It's too tall for dining and these edges make it inefficient as a war table."

The other two join me and the three of us study the table. I run a hand over the surface. The texture of the fabric is soft with a short pile.

"It's a pool table," a young blonde girl says, stepping in to join us. She skips down the two steps into the room and bounces on the balls of her feet as she makes her way over. "It's a game to pass the time."

The female is an adolescent Elbirfae with the same white wings as the warrior, Tundra. "Are you Tundra's offspring?"

She looks at me and laughs. "No. More like his little sister. I grew up in the same community and when our people were killed, he found me and took me in. I'm Skye."

"Will you show us how this table game works?" Beta asks, pointing at the table. "We have time to pass and are unsure what to do with ourselves."

"Sure, I can try. My boyfriend, Yarko, is much better than I am." She hustles around the corner of the table and grabs several polished sticks. After handing us each one, she bends down and starts retrieving hard balls from the far end of the table. After corralling them into a wooden triangle, she pushes the grouping to a point on the soft surface and then removes the triangle. "So, this is traditionally a parlor game from the Human Realm. You play as individuals or partners and the winner is the first person who hits this white ball into the others and sinks all their designated balls into any of the six pockets around the table."

"How do I know which balls I'm to sink?" Alpha asks.

"That's determined after the first ball sinks. Or, since there are three of you, you can choose a set of numbers one to five, six to ten, and eleven to fifteen."

"But what is the purpose of this game?" I ask.

She shrugs. "To spend time with your friends and see who can read the angles and bounces best? It's just for fun."

"Fun," Beta repeats.

She nods, passing a strange gaze over the three of us. "You know... fun. To entertain yourselves and enjoy your time together."

I look at the fragile stick. "And there's no hitting people with these?"

She barks a laugh. "No. No hitting. Here, I'll show you."

Taking the stick she handed to Alpha, she grabs the loose white ball and walks to the far end of the table. "You set the white ball anywhere here, and then you strike it with the padded tip of your cue and force it to hit the other balls. You have one turn unless one of your balls falls into a pocket. If it does, you get to go again. If it doesn't, your turn is over and it's the next person's turn."

Beta follows her to the far end of the table and bends as she does, looking at the cluster of balls with a knowing smile. "This is a test of geometry, trigonometry, and physics. We shall do very well at this game."

She shows us how to hold the stick and the motion of how

to strike the white ball and then lets us try. "You don't want to hit it so hard you knock the ball off the table, but you also don't want to hit it so softly that it doesn't travel the distance and hit anything at all."

"Because if I don't hit anything it's a wasted turn," Beta says.

Skye smiles. "That's right. There are distinct challenges you can play, but for now, why don't you practice your shots and learn how to bounce the balls off the rails? Then, when Yarko gets here later, he can tell you about the other objectives."

I examine the stick I've been given and test it's weight and balance. "Thank you, Skye. Despite your comment to the contrary, you are very knowledgeable about this pastime. Would you care to join us in playing?"

I fully expect the young thing to say no. After all, we are highly dangerous, genetically enhanced soldiers, but she doesn't seem daunted.

"Sure. We can be partners and they can be the other team," she says, selecting a stick for herself. "I'll start, so you can see how this goes." Pressing her hand against the fuzzy, gold surface of the table, she pulls back her stick and then jabs it forward, striking the ball and forcing it to hit the others.

The contact creates a satisfying 'clack' sound and then the balls burst free of their positions. As we watch, the balls bounce and roll until a completely blue ball drops into the leather pouch on the corner of the table.

The girl smiles triumphantly. "Okay, I got a solid blue ball in. That means my partner and I are shooting the solid balls, and you two are shooting the striped balls."

"And you get another turn because you sunk a ball," Beta says.

"Exactly." The girl walks around the table and lines up her next shot. "And each time, you realign your shot to shoot the white ball into your target. Now that it is determined that I'm shooting solids, I have to hit a solid ball."

Honestly, the entire premise of the game seems frivolous and unimportant, but I admit, I enjoy studying the table and calculating the angles and possibilities of the next shot.

Skye fails to sink anything on her next attempt and so straightens and points to Alpha and me. "Okay, so who wants their turn next?"

I grip my stick and smile. "I think I would like to take a turn."

"Excellent. Then step right up and try it."

~

Mac

TUNDRA and I are sitting at the long, elaborately carved table, when Shift and Flash bring Lark into the dining room. Her gait is a little stiff and slower than usual, but all-in-all, she's upright and has a great deal more color in her cheeks than she did last night.

In fact, she looks downright flushed.

And she smells... Well, they *all* smell aroused.

My cat prowls within me, letting off a long slow growl. I cut that shit off as soon as I can but Tundra definitely noticed.

He casts me a sympathetic look and stands. "May I get the three of you something to eat?"

Lark presses a hand on her stomach. "I would appreciate anything you have in the kitchen. Thank you. I'm not fussy, but I am famished."

"Take a seat. I have a pot of hot jarangon stew on the stove. I'll be right back." He gestures to the table and I gather the maps of the compound layout and the lists of names we were poring over.

"Yer lookin' better, lass. Did Shift here cure all yer ills, then?" The comment comes out with a little more force than I intended, but there's no helping it. With this fucking bonding pull thrumming through my bloodstream and directing the flow of that stream straight to my cock, that the three of them reek of arousal is offensive to my dominant Sith side.

Thankfully, they don't seem to pick up on my annoyance. Or if they do, they're smart enough to let it die a quiet death.

"What are you working on?" Lark asks.

"Tundra and I were reviewin' his plans for bringin' the Amberloq applicants for the warrior trials. They're set to arrive in two days, and since yer one of the Amberloq Generals, I assume yer stayin' here fer the proceedings."

"Yes, I told Dune and Tundra I want to help them with that. Rebuilding the Amberloq force is a priority for quadrant security."

"Right, so if yer stayin' then I suppose these boys are stayin', which means we're roomies for the next few days. How cozy."

Her gaze shifts from Flash to Shift and then back to me. "I suppose that's true."

"Here you are," Tundra says, carrying in a large tray with four soldier-sized bowls of stew. "There is plenty more in the pot. I turned off the element, but it will stay warm for a few hours at least. The water in the taps is mountain fresh, but if you prefer, we filled the refrigerator with ale."

"You're welcome," Dune says, leaning into the dining room and hanging off the frame of the door. "Come on, Frosty, the party's started. Get the lead out. This is your one and only roundup."

Tundra arches a dark brow and shakes his head. "If you'll excuse us. Princess Honor and our other mate, Shadow, arrived a short time ago, and we are eager to give them the tour and settle in. They can only stay one night and we want to spend time with them."

I chuckle. "Take yer time, warrior. Today is about rest and recuperation after a tough fight."

Tundra nods. "If you need anything, just—"

"—figure it out or find it yourself," Dune finishes for him. "No offense, people, but we'll be busy for a few hours. And when I say we'll be busy, I mean we'll be *getting* busy... if Tundra ever gets his ass in gear."

Tundra rolls his eyes and wipes a hand over his flushed cheeks. "And that is my cue, because if I don't leave now, he'll just get worse."

Turning on his heels with a flare of his stunning ebony-flecked white wings, the Icy Peaks Biome General strides out of the expansive dining hall, head held high and Dune reaching around to smack his ass.

Flash unloads the bowls from the tray and distributes them as Lark hands everyone a spoon.

"I would like a tour of this facility too," Flash says. "Do you think I could join them after our meal?"

Lark pulls her spoon from her mouth and chews as she shakes her head. "No, sweetie. Dune said they were taking a tour, but what he wasn't saying was they are planning the same thing you are for after lunch."

"They want to join with you?"

I choke on my stew and launch to my feet, heading to the fridge. Ale sounds pretty good right now. Pounding my chest as I walk, it takes a couple of rasping coughs to stop choking and settle down.

When I return to the table, I set down four bottles. "Sorry about that."

"Connor Mac?" Shift asks, accepting his drink. "What are your expectations for our relationship? Will you be joining only with me, or would you like to be naked with Lark and my brothers as well?"

I stop dead, blinking at the man. "I'm sorry? What's that now?"

The feminine giggle across the table has my brain spinning. "Sorry. That's likely my fault. The boys and I were having a conversation earlier about intimacy and lovers. I mentioned it's important to understand the expectations of your sex partner so that no misunderstandings occur and no trust is broken."

I tip back the bottle and let the icy brew glug over my tongue and down my throat. If there is any luck in this world, this is a magical intoxicating fae ale that will erase this conversation from my memory.

"Well? Would you like to join with Lark?" Shift asks, glancing between the two of us. "She is kind, very soft, and makes the most intoxicating noises when being pleasured."

Lark chokes and flushes beat red.

"She also said the five of us are in a relationship."

Lark sets her spoon down and picks up her napkin, using it to shield herself while she regains her composure. "Context matters, you two."

She takes another moment to pull herself together and when she meets my gaze, her cheeks are all kinds of flushed. "We were talking about understanding expectations from lovers, and I *actually* said we couldn't speak for you and that, for the moment, the five of us are bound. I said it was important to respect everyone's wishes, however that works."

I take another long drink. "Can we please change the subject?"

Lark lets out a long breath. "Yes, please."

Shift frowns. "I don't understand. Why won't you tell us your expectations? Lark said it was important, so we don't break trust with people we care about."

Feckin' hell. I set the bottle onto the table and froth rises inside. "I understand everythin' is new to ye, lad, and I'm tryin' to keep that in mind, honestly, but I haven't got any answers fer ye. I'm a soldier fer a company that works out of the Human Realm. I have a home and a life in another world that has nothin' to do with the job I'm doin' here. Aye, I feel the pull, but that doesn't mean I need to give in to it."

"But in the forest—"

"Just because I lost my grip and we had one frenzied moment doesn't mean we're in a relationship and honestly, puttin' me on the spot in front of Lark and the others serves no purpose other than makin' me want to hit the road."

"But we're on a mountain. There is no road."

I groan and stand, the legs of my chair scraping as I rise. "I don't want to appear insensitive or rude here, but feckin' hell, man, one fuck in the forest doesn't mean we're in a relationship."

I see the light of expectation in his eyes go out and I hate myself for being the one who caused it. I just don't know what else to say or do.

Grabbing one of the other ales off the table, I turn and stomp away, my boots beating out a steady rhythm. "Feckin' hell."

CHAPTER EIGHT

Shift

Watching Connor Mac storm off with his fists clenched at his side, his boots striking out an angry rhythm, and his Sith cat letting off a threatening growl, makes my insides hurt. Flash described to me earlier how he felt when Lark was injured and I think I understand. "Caring for people is hard."

"Yes, it is." Lark shifts her seat closer to me, wraps her wing around my shoulders, and her arm around my back. The warmth of her wing feels protective, and it doesn't escape my attention that Lark is becoming as protective of us as we are of her. "I'm sorry you're hurting, but relationships aren't always easy."

"Then, if it hurts like this, why do people do it?"

Her thumb brushes gently against my arm as she rests her head on my shoulder. "Because when the fighting is over and you work through the problems, being in love is worth it."

I search through my data banks and there's nothing substantial for me to access. While they made us to interact with the members of the quadrant and possibly even integrate with them in covert data collection, they did not intend us to form attachments or relationships.

Does that mean our program is faulty or was it merely incomplete?

"Have you been in love before?" Flash is leaning toward us from across the table and the adoration in his eyes is easy to read.

I hope his affections are never rejected, like mine have been with Connor Mac.

Lark pats my arm and straightens in her seat. "No. I was always more of a warrior than females were expected to be in my biome. While the other girls were decorating their feathers with gems and sparkly chains, I was saving my credits for battle armor. The males didn't find that sexy."

Flash shakes his head. "Fools, the lot of them. They obviously lacked in intelligence because the idea of you having battle armor on your wings is nothing but sexy."

She chuckles and looks at me. "The important thing to remember is that none of us have been in love before, so navigating deep feelings and the talk of bonding and forever is new and intimidating. Even though Mac was upset, he told us some important concerns of his—valid concerns—and we should think about them."

I meet her gaze, replaying the conversation in my mind. "He has a life apart from us in a realm where we are not welcome."

She picks up her spoon and gestures for us to resume eating our meal. "Right. So, let's try to understand how he feels."

"He is angry that I want to claim him." I push my spoon through the chunky medley of meat and vegetables.

"I think it's more about frustration."

Flash swallows and opens a bottle of ale. "It seemed like

anger. His heart rate was elevated, his facial coloration intensi-fied, his voice grew louder—"

Lark raises her hand. "I understand the science, but let's think about the man. He said he has a life in another realm and being with us would change everything for him."

"It would change everything for you as well, and yet you don't seem angry with us."

I study her facial cues and Flash is right. Lark doesn't seem angry about the prospect of our bond at all. "It doesn't anger you to change the course of your life for us?"

She sets her hand on the top of my leg and sighs. "No, sweetie, because some awful people destroyed the life I knew two years ago. Until a few months ago, I was a prisoner with no life other than trying to survive and to keep the people around me alive."

Flash's gaze grows tight and his jaw flexes. "If those who tortured you weren't already dead, I would kill them myself."

Lark nods. "Thank you. I slayed my own demons, but I appreciate the thought."

I take another bite of food. The taste doesn't register and when I swallow it feels like a congealed lump sliding down my throat and weighing heavy in my stomach.

Lark must see my discomfort because she takes the open ale in front of Flash and holds it for me to take. "Drink up."

"It won't help."

"It won't hurt."

I do as she suggests and take a few long swallows. The cool tang of the liquid doesn't help the ache in my chest, but it quenches my thirst.

"Okay, so back to Mac," she says. "Think about this situation from his perspective. He's a squadron leader, and he both loves his job and takes great pride in it. He's likely worked his entire adult life building the respect of his team and if he accepts the situation with his bonding with you, and by extension with all of us, means the end of that."

That sounds upsetting.

"I thought it was simply that he resents my claim on him."

She shrugs. "I can't say that has nothing to do with it, but try to remember Mac is an alpha male. Shifters live with a second entity within them. His cat is dominant and aggressive. The two of them are used to being in charge of their life and their choices."

Flash opens another of the bottles and tosses the cap onto the table. "His cat is fearsome."

Lark nods. "And no matter your intention, you claiming him because of the pull of your shared attraction threatens to take away his choice. It probably makes him angry."

"But I did not initiate the pull. It's happening to me as well."

"I know that, and more importantly, *he* knows that. It's just been a really stressful couple of days. Let's leave him to breathe and take things at his own speed, and we'll work on integrating the three—or I guess with Alpha and Beta it's the five of you—into realm life."

I swallow, pleased that the pressure in my chest has eased a little. Gesturing to Lark and Flash's empty bowls, I meet my brother's gaze. "Tundra said there was more food in the pot on the stove. The two of you should get a second helping. Our lady's hungers are still our priority."

Flash nods and rises, collecting both bowls before striking off to replenish their portions.

When Lark and I are alone, she rests her head on my shoulder once more. The sensation of closeness is alien but lovely. It's a comfort I've never felt before her. "Mac will come around. You'll see. Give him a little time and a little space."

~

Lark

AFTER FLASH and I finish our second bowls of stew, the three of us wander the main floor of the house, exploring our temporary home. The Amberloq warrior trials will begin in a few days and there is much to get done before the applicants arrive.

"How many prospective warriors are you expecting?" Flash asks as we make our way past a room with a massive square table in the center of the space.

"The last time I heard, there were the twenty kids and ten to fifteen independent applicants. With you three, Beta, and Alpha, it'll be thirty or more."

Shift seems surprised by that. "We are to take part in the warrior trials?"

"I think you should. I doubt anyone will question your abilities, but if you are to fight among the Amberloq, it would be good to understand the process of their training and what is expected beyond proficiency in battle."

"By that definition, will you be joining the trials as well, my lovely?" Flash asks me. "You mentioned before that Tundra and Dune completed the warrior training and were inducted into the Amberloq years before the Thornebane rule was overthrown. You learned much in your years as a prisoner, but if understanding the process of their training is an asset, then you might wish to join us as well."

My mouth falls open. I hadn't thought about it like that. "Let me speak to Tundra and Dune about that. You're right, of course, but if the Biome Generals are meant to instill a sense of standard, I'm not sure I want my weaknesses known by all the applicants."

Flash seems to consider that. "I think you have a point. We will train you privately and you can oversee the procedures as a leader of the program."

I nod. "I think so too, but I'll speak to Tundra and Dune about it, anyway."

The gleeful squeal of a young girl catches our attention and prompts us to continue our exploration. Following the deep rumble of muffled male voices, we turn down a long hall.

The *clack* and *crack* of what could only be balls on a pool table give me a better idea of where we're going and what we're looking for.

We follow the sounds of laughter until we find Link, Beta, Alpha, and a young snowy peaks female I know and love dearly —Skye.

"Bank, bank, side." Link indicates where his shot will engage with the table.

I hold up my hand to halt Flash and Shift and give him a moment to line up his shot. When he strikes the white ball and it sends the other balls in a scramble across the table, the ball he targeted does indeed bank twice before dropping into the side pocket.

Skye lets off another squeal of delight and then she runs over and meets Link in a choreographed sequence of hand gestures they seem to have developed as a sign of unified triumph.

When they're finished, she gifts him with a smile that is so open and unguarded. I can't believe she's even dealing with the male I've been butting heads with for the past three days.

Except... one look at him tells me he's *not* that man, for he not only returns her affectionate grin, he winks at her, laughing as she bounces over to bump knuckles with Alpha and Beta.

Where did this man come from?

Because he isn't any iteration of the Link I know.

These boys never cease to surprise me.

Somehow, despite Andras Brass building what he thought were the optimum stone-cold killing machines, Flash, Shift, and possibly even Link, have grown past their programing.

The three are budding into thoughtful, caring males. Five minutes ago, if someone would've told me I'd be saying that about Link, I would've bet every credit in my savings vault they were crazy.

And all it took was the unending optimism and sweet sass of Skye.

"Lark! You're here. How are you?" Skye bounds over and I hug her close. "Tundra said you were hurt. Are you fixed now?" She steps back and looks me over.

"Shift and Lukas healed me."

"Lukas is the magic man, after all." She grins at Shift and Flash flanking me and then thrusts her hand forward. "Hi, I'm Skye."

"Hello, Skye," Shift says, working up the first smile I've seen on him since Mac stormed off.

"Skye was with me in the goblin camp and then, as fate would have it, Tundra rescued us. She thought he'd been killed when the other soldiers were assassinated, but he and Dune were here."

Skye nods. "If everything happens for a reason, then saving their lives, falling in love, and creating our family was the fae universe's big plan."

"It certainly all worked out in the end." I meet Shift's gaze and send him a knowing smile. "Things almost always do."

"Do you want to play with us?" Skye asks. "Come on, we'll show you. It's fun, isn't it guys?"

The three soldiers nod.

Leave it to Skye to play the part of super soldier liaison. "You boys play for a bit. I'm going to see if there is anything other than ale in the refrigerator. I'll swing back around for you in a little while."

With that, I leave them to socialize and head out to do exactly what I counseled Shift not to do.

Find Mac to talk some sense into him.

Searching for Mac through the halls of the Amberloq Mount Nekko retreat is a futile effort in hide-and-seek. Only, I don't think he's actually hiding and I'm not sure I'm actually seeking.

Because now that the world around me is quiet and I think through my advice, I'm pretty sure I should let sleeping dogs lay... or, in this case, brooding cats.

So, after exploring close to two dozen rooms on the main floor and following the winding staircase down to another long run of rooms in the lower level, I take the first set of double doors leading outside to abandon the search and get some fresh air.

Seriously, what made me think I have any sage relationship advice to offer? I've only had a few dates and none of them were worth repeating.

I wander across a vast, flat training ground and wonder if this is where Tundra and Dune plan to hold the trials. Mac likely knows because he was working out the logistics with Tundra before we interrupted and sent him storming off.

Maybe I shouldn't have gotten involved in what was happening between him and Shift.

Maybe I shouldn't have brought up needing to iron out expectations so soon.

Maybe there shouldn't be expectations when no one knows what's happening or how it will affect us in the long term.

I walk to the edge of the training field and stand at the stone wall that divides the compound from the sheer drop to the mountainside below. The barrier rises above my head and I wonder if it's ensuring warriors in training don't get flipped down the side of the mountain while fighting.

Flapping my wings, I lift my feet off the ground and fly forward enough to sit on the wide stone ledge. When I lower myself down to sit, I lean forward and whistle into the vacuous space.

Wow, not the place to be if someone has a fear of heights.

Then again, Elbirfae have wings, so there's no reason for concern.

I squint, staring at the shadows and crevices stretching for miles below. It's impossible to estimate how high up we are because night is taking over the sky and there isn't enough light to judge the distance.

CHAPTER NINE

Mac

"That bad, is it?" I take a running leap to scale the eight-foot stone wall barricading the training grounds from the jagged rock face below. I land on the ledge with the balance and skill of my Sith cat and stroll along the top surface like an alley cat on the back fence. "Are ye thinkin' it'll be easier to jump and take yer chances?"

When I lean over the expanse to take in the sheer drop below, fear spikes in the air and in those gemstone-green eyes of hers in equal measure.

Is she worried about me?

I force my expression to show no sign of humor—even though the idea that I might fall over the edge is ridiculous.

To ease her concern, I crouch on the ledge beside her and take a seat, letting my legs swing loose. The tension in her frame eases, and the sweet scent of her relief replaces the bitter tang of her worry. "Ye needn't fash, little bird. I'm not ready to end it all just yet."

"That's good to hear."

Silence settles between us and my mind drifts through everything that's happened over the past week—the good, the bad, and the ugly. "I'm sorry if I overreacted in the kitchen earlier. I didn't mean to make a scene or draw ye into things."

She chuckles. "With everything the two of us have been through the past week, I'm the last person you need to apologize to. Besides, I think I've made a few scenes in front of you since my rescue."

Aye, that's true.

It's taken her a bit to find her footing, but I don't hold that against her. She lost everyone she loved, her home, her purpose, and then, even though us rescuing her was a good thing, she lost the world she'd rebuilt when we pulled her out of that goblin prison camp last month. I don't fault her for being angry.

The two of us sit there for a long moment, watching the last of the tangerine glow drop behind the deep purple peaks of the surrounding mountains.

"I shouldn't have spoken to Shift about your place in this relationship mess," she says, brushing bits of stone and dirt from her palm. "It's all so messy. I'm sorry if I made things harder for you."

I sigh. "Och, lass, ye didn't. Yer tryin' to navigate the minefield yer in as well. And I'd even go further than it bein' messy and say it's a clusterfuck."

She laughs. "Try to remember that they don't understand any more than we do about what is happening. I'd even say less."

I drop my chin and exhale a heavy breath. "Aye, I realize that too."

I understand she wants to stand as the champion for the three. She did much the same thing with the Elbirfae prisoners in that camp. She's the type of person who stands strong and takes the hits while others can't. It's commendable, really.

"If it helps, I think you were justified."

I cast her a sidelong glance. "In what sense?"

"Because no matter what's at play here, you shouldn't be guilted or forced into caring for Shift. If you don't feel the connection like he does, you have every right to stop him from hoping and walk away."

Her comment couldn't be further from the truth. I feel the connection. I feel it so keenly it's driving me crazy. It twists in my guts and burns in my cock. It's a burst of lust deep in my balls and a pressure in my chest driving me to claim his mouth, touch his skin, and mark him with my cum.

My cat has taken the primal call and grown wild with it. He wants nothing more than to clamp my teeth into the meaty flesh of Shift's shoulder and to claim him as my mate.

But I'm more than a wild beast.

Everything I said to Shift was the truth. I have a life beyond this realm—a life I love. Despite seeing how the whole fated mate magic worked out for Hawk and Lukas, I can't just blindly submit and hope for the same outcome—I won't.

With the sun down, a chill settles over us and I realize Lark's skin is raised with goosebumps. I rub my hands over her arm to build some friction. "Why don't ye head back inside and find the boys? Yer cold and it won't do fer ye to get sick with all that's comin' at us in the next few days."

She draws a long breath and smiles. "You're welcome to join us, but I totally understand if you prefer to keep your distance."

I lift a shoulder. "I'm not sure keepin' my distance will do any good. It's more about tryin' to clear my head so I can make a conscious decision instead of bein' driven by the madness of the pull."

She rests a hand on my wrist. "I'm sorry you're going through this."

"I could say the same."

Lark shrugs. "Our situations are unique. I've got nothing to lose and am alone. The idea of having three incredibly sexy, strong, brave males devoted to me doesn't sound that bad."

I chuckle. "When ye put it that way, I'd have to agree. Although Link is a bit of a wildcard."

She laughs. "No kidding."

"Don't let yer guard down completely, little bird. Ye've been through a lot and I want ye to be right about these boys, but we still can't be sure we know all the parts of this puzzle are on the board."

She nods. "I promise to keep my eyes open and remain objective as long as possible. Though I'm excited to discover why the universe has given me this opportunity."

"Weel, maybe after all the universe took from ye, it's decided ye deserve a good dose of happiness."

She waggles her ebony eyebrows at me. "And a good dose of sex. I definitely deserve that."

The snarl of my cat echoes over our shared consciousness, but I don't let on. I don't get to play it both ways. Either Shift is mine or he's not. And even if he is, there's a bond between Lark and the three of them as well. I don't get to be territorial about that.

Thankfully, Sith shifters crave the camaraderie of having a pack. I've always filled that need with my military squad, but now things are changing.

Lark twists at the waist and swings her leg to get up. Instinctually, I roll backward, kick my feet over my head, and drop to my boots. Raising my hand, I offer to help her down. "I wish ye well in yer pursuit of happiness. And please, if he's upset, just maybe say I need a bit of time."

There's no need to clarify who the 'he' in that statement is. Lark nods. "Don't stay out in the cold too long, soldier."

I hear the subtext in her comment and nod. "Not a second more than is necessary, I promise."

Lark

MAC HELPS me down from the high wall, which is gentlemanly, but unnecessary. I have wings, after all. Still, he's looking more relaxed than when we were all in the kitchen earlier and I consider our time out here well spent. As I walk toward the sliding glass doors, I spot Flash waiting inside and offer him a smile. "I take it you came looking for me?"

"Your prolonged absence made me uncomfortable, and I wished to see that you were well and happy."

I lean forward and place a kiss on his cheek. "I missed you too."

That seems to go a long way in making him feel better. "It seems your private conversation went well."

I study his face, as I often do, to read if there is any subtext behind his comment. There isn't. Flash isn't jealous or worried or even prying. He's simply making an observation. "Yes. I wanted to check in with him and apologize in case I overstepped earlier when discussing our expectations of this relationship."

He frowns. "You did not overstep. Trying to help us all find our place with one another is welcome and necessary. I hope Mac told you as much."

I press my palm to his cheek. "He did."

The moment my hand touches his skin, he stiffens and turns the table on me. His hand shoots forward to cup the side of my neck and then he locks gazes with me. "Are you well, my lovely? Your skin doesn't hold it's usual warmth, but your pupils are equal and reactive and your pulse is strong and steady."

I chuckle, gripping his wrist to move his hand from my neck to my lips. After placing a gentle kiss against the center of his palm, I step against his chest and wrap my arms around his ribs.

Skin-to-skin contact enhances Flash's ability to read my thoughts and emotions. With that in mind, I answer his question with as much anticipation and mental imaging as I can manage. "I'm fine. Although, you're right. It was chilly outside. How would you like to spend some private time with me and warm me up? I never got my hungers sated."

His eyes flash with a sudden spark. "I would enjoy that very much. Should we invite Shift? He was the one you wanted to join with earlier."

"And you're sure that doesn't bother you?"

He shakes his head, his expression open and honest. "Not at all."

Well, I won't say no to that.

"Then we should definitely go find him and invite him to join us. I found a room on this floor that has a lovely fireplace and some oversized couches. I think warming up in front of the fire would be a wonderful way to spend the next few hours."

Flash takes my hand and then gestures for me to lead the way. "Take me to your fireplace room and I will invite Shift over our neuro-link. That way I can warm your skin right away."

"I like the sound of that."

The two of us wander through the lower level of the building for a moment while I get my bearings and then I find the room I was talking about.

It's a large recreation room with a two-sided fireplace in the center of the floor. It sits about three-quarters of the way toward the far wall, dividing the space and providing the illusion of two smaller spaces.

On this side of the room—the three-quarter side—they position three oversized couches in a U facing the fireplace. And on the other side of the fireplace, there is a long bar stretching wall-to-wall with half a dozen leather stools in front of it, as if we were in an actual tavern ready to be served.

"What do you think?" I ask Flash, striding over toward the fireplace to figure out how to turn it on.

Flash's gaze blanks out and then his attention snaps back to the moment, and he passes me to look at the selection of alcohol. "Did you know that part of our society adaptation programming is being able to order and make drinks?"

"No, but I'm looking forward to putting that information to the test. Come, make me a drink while we wait for Shift and the room warms up."

The two of us walk around the stone fireplace into the area where the bar is set up. Even though it's part of the entire room, it feels like a private little nook. I climb onto one of the leather bar stools and Flash steps in behind the bar.

"You know, you're the sexiest bartender I've ever had serving me." I eye him up and down.

Between the fact that they seem allergic to shirts and have the finest, chiseled upper bodies, blond hair, and caramel gold eyes, it almost hurts to look at one of them, and then there are two.

Shift arrives, and he looks all kinds of sinful and sexy as he takes in the two of us. He steps in beside me, runs a hand across my skin, and caresses the root of my wing where it connects with my back.

My eyes roll back in my head as I groan. "I'm not sure if you're aware of this," I say, swallowing to keep from moaning out loud, "but that is an incredibly sensitive erogenous zone for an Elbirfae female."

The throaty chuckle accompanying Shift's smile tells me he is very aware of what he's doing.

"Just how detailed is your knowledge of seduction techniques?" I ask.

He presses his mouth against my temple. "More of our systems and backup data files are coming online by the moment. I think you'll be pleasantly surprised at the upgrades in our understanding."

I'm not sure if I'm hearing what I want to hear, but I'd swear there was a sexual innuendo in that statement. I turn to meet his heated gaze, his lips just a breath away from mine. "Are you sure everything's all right? You don't have to front with me if you're still upset about Mac."

He shakes his head and the corner of his mouth lifts in a crooked smile. "One has nothing to do with the other. If you remember, you and I were about to explore our carnal desires before our conversation with Connor Mac."

"True, but I, uh... it seemed like he was your focused attraction until now."

He takes my hand, guides it down the rippled plain of his abdomen, and over the fabric of his pants. The solid length of his erection beneath my palm says my observation isn't accurate. "I have felt the warmth of you being our catalyst and the rightness of you being ours from the beginning. I'm sorry if my focus and confusion about Connor Mac didn't make that clear."

I swallow and meet the warm swirl of those caramel eyes of his. "No need to apologize. I just want to be sure we all know what's happening here."

He closes the distance between our mouths and pivots my barstool, so I'm facing him. With his free hand and a step forward, he opens my knees and steps in close, pulling me to the edge of the seat with him between my legs.

As his mouth moves over mine, it's like a dam is bursting free. His kiss is smoldering, his mouth claiming mine with every brush of lips and swipe of tongue.

My hands slide around his ribs, pulling him tighter into my embrace until I'm crushing our bodies together. His fingers tighten, holding me in place, one hand laced into the back of my hair and the other against my back, brushing the roots of my wings.

I'm washed with the magic of his gift and my cells come alive. Where Flash's ability to share and read emotions is intimate and unites us more than I can explain, Shift's gifts of molecular restoration seem to seep into my body and breathe life into my cells.

I break the kiss for a breath, my head spinning.

Whatever his most recent unlocking of files entailed, I'm wholeheartedly enjoying the result. None of them seem nearly as stiff or unsure as they have over the past few days.

And the new confidence is hot as hell.

"Do you want your drink, my lovely?" Flash says, laughter in his voice. He's leaning over the bar, watching Shift and I make out, hunger flaring in his eyes.

I reach over, take possession of the drink and swallow it down in a rush of hurried swallows. It's fruity and sweet and way too delicious. "Thank you. That quenched my thirst. Now let's move on to my hunger."

CHAPTER TEN

Shift

*L*ark makes her needs known and I am more than happy to comply. Our female is hungry. That's fitting because I am too. It's shameful that she thought my only interest in our relationship lay with Connor Mac. Yes, the pull I'm feeling for him is a constant tug, but the bond I feel for Lark is a hot wanton simmering low in my core.

Sliding my hands down her sides, I find the top of her pants and the front fastener. Pushing the metal tab through the mooring, I open things up and loosen the fabric keeping me from where I need to be.

"If there's anything you want me to do more, less, or differently, tell me. I want our joining to feed everything you hunger for."

"How can a girl go wrong with that?"

"Flash, help me get our female naked. I fear that if I don't get at her skin quickly, I might just shred her clothes and leave her with nothing to wear."

Flash chuckles and joins me from behind the bar. "If that happened, she would need to stay sealed away in our quarters to keep me from slashing the throats of any Amberloq trainees who might think to look at what is ours. With our expectations set, I admit I feel rather murderous about anyone from outside our bond casting their eyes upon her."

I nip her bottom lip and grin. "As do I. However, keeping her naked and sealed away in our quarters doesn't sound like such a bad thing."

Lark laughs in my arms and shoves her pants and silky bottoms down her toned thighs. Flash takes a knee to undo her boots and work her pants off, while I unfasten the sides of her shirt and push the fabric over her head and beyond her wings.

"That is much better," I say, taking in Lark's warm, tanned skin. I want to touch her, want to explore every inch of her skin with my fingertips, tongue, and body.

She is soft flesh over hardened muscle, generous curves of hips and breast next to toned plains of belly and back. I find the contradictions entrancing.

"May I?" I hold my hand, cupped over the round of her breasts, and wait for her to answer.

"Of course. Please."

After working at healing her for hours yesterday, I grew a familiar sense of her curves and the warmth of her body. But during that time, I was healing her and had no intention of betraying her trust. Now, with her consent, I have every intention of taking in all the sights and sensations.

I trace a feather-light finger along the edge of her nipple and watch as the dark nub pinches in response. When I rub my thumb over the tipped peak, Lark groans and arches into my touch.

It doesn't take me long to read her body's reaction and learn the nuances of how she likes to be caressed. With my thumb stroking over the sensitive tip, I test the weight of her breast in my palm. "Your breasts are incredible."

"Absolutely." Flash has finished with her boots and pants and is still on his knees. Stroking his hand up the silky column of her leg, he rides the gentle curves of her muscles up to the fleshy round of her bottom. "All her parts are amazing."

Lark chuckles before me, and I realize we're doing more information gathering than joining. Cupping the round globes of her backside, I lift her against my body. Her legs wrap around my hips without hesitation and I revel in her trust. "Enough commentary on your body parts. I wish to talk less and join more."

"I love a man with a plan."

Turning the two of us away from the bar, I press her back against the stone side wall of the massive fireplace and reclaim her kiss.

The passion we share each time we touch reignites the moment our lips meet. The feminine groan that rumbles at the back of her throat amplifies my desire.

She grabs onto my shoulders as my cock brushes the wet folds at her core. That our bodies line up so perfectly is more proof that she is ours and that we were meant for her. Her fingers grow rough, gripping the muscles of my shoulders, and pulling me closer as if frustrated.

I answer that heightened need by accepting her invitation. Thrusting inside her... deep inside the warmth of her body, something inside me shifts.

This is...

She gasps and I grow still, needing a moment for my systems to recalibrate. The sensation of her body's moist heat accepting me is so profoundly indescribable, I almost forget to breathe.

Lark quivers in my arms and I feel the quake of her response clenching around the flesh of my stiff cock. "Oh, gods, you fill me so good."

It's true. It takes a moment for my sensors to catch up, but she's right because her inner muscles are surrounding me and squeezing me with such intense possession, I can't imagine a tighter or more spectacular fit. "It's incredible."

"And now you move, brother," Flash says, looking at me with a heated smile. "The sensations are even better as you withdraw almost to the point of leaving her and then push back in again."

I follow Flash's suggestion once... twice...

My heart rate multiplies and all my systems...

I stop thrusting, clutching Lark against me, my entire system overloading with the bombardment of pleasure. It's too much.

"I don't know how to sort through all these feelings and sensations." I close my eyes and try to rein in the chaos of my body, mind, and emotions, feeding me input all at once. When my senses come back online, I meet Lark's heated gaze. "My apologies."

She brushes her lips against mine. "Don't you dare apologize. If you need to take a moment to savor the feel of things and sort through how that makes you feel, then take your moment. With you inside me, I'm certainly not complaining."

Wait until you she orgasms around you... and you find your climax... it just keeps getting better, Flash says directly into my mind.

I can't imagine anything better than this, but with Flash's prompting, I withdraw to the length of my arousal, and then push back inside until I'm firmly seated inside her again.

Like before, the pleasure threatens to short out my sensory receptors.

Again, Flash says. *More thrusting, faster. Her body will milk your cock and the friction will cause her inner muscles to build the pressure of her release. Make her come. It's spectacular.*

I do as he suggests and thrust again and again. The silky glide of our joining... the sound of our bodies slapping together… the bounce of her breasts each time I'm buried to the hilt…

The pleasure of it steals my breath. She is as hungry as I am, demanding I go deeper, harder, faster.

Her fingers dig into my skin, clutching me and crushing us together as her inner muscles tighten and grip me just as Flash said they would.

Lark's wings flare out behind her against the stone and with her eyes closed and a look of bliss on her face, she is the most beautiful thing I've ever seen.

"You feel… so good…" she gasps, her words punctuated by a gasp as I stroke her insides. "So good. Kiss me too. I want your mouth."

I lean in and reclaim her lips, growling as both of us grow more frenzied. Sweat blooms on her skin. As she throws her head back, the golden light of the fireplace creates a glistening glow over her body.

Even that sparks another pang of desperation.

"I want to be joined like this forever," I say, my control waning as I thrust her against the unforgiving stone of the fireplace wall. I swear I hear a few of them crack, but I don't care and Lark doesn't seem to notice. And there's no way I can stop.

The frenzy of her need and my ecstasy are transcendent, and then… I access my heightened gift.

Molecular realignment.

With a focus on her pleasure, I grow my cock four percent in width and length and choose a vibrational speed to massage her most intimate longings.

"Oh, Shift!" Lark shouts, her voice a throaty rasp. "What did you—"

A frenzy of pure need consumes her, and she grows even more carnal. As I thrust inside her in a wild and rough rhythm, she pants, her fingernails biting into the flesh of my backside. "Yes! Oh, yes, Shift."

Her insides are greedy, gripping my cock, tightening around me. It's like being plugged directly into pleasure and having it consume you. It only takes a few more hammering thrusts, and she throws her head back and her body arches in my arms.

Her expression is rapt, locked in an intense, yet exquisite moment in time. Suspended in my arms, her body convulses. Her back arches in a beautiful line that pushes her hard-tipped breasts out at me.

Having her pulse around me and watching her come apart in my arms detonates the burn that's been building deep in my groin. My breathing hitches and I cry out as my hips falter in rhythm and then lock and I spill my release inside her.

Wave after wave of pleasure rushes through me and into her. The connection I thought I felt for her before is nothing to how I feel now.

My female.

The two of us remain clutched as one body, and our breathing settles. My bliss ebbs, settling into a warm contentment, and then my attention returns once more to Lark.

She seems to have lost herself completely and I tense, worried she's suffering. But no, other than her heart rate racing, all her vital signs are strong.

Beautiful, Flash says in my mind.

Agreed.

"That was incredible." My words fall off my tongue as a true benediction.

"Yes, it was." Lark unwraps her legs as if I'm supposed to put her down.

"Oh, no, my female." I keep my hold on her body and stride around the fireplace to several wide, comfortable-looking couches. "We are not finished with you yet, are we Flash?"

Flash chuckles beside me and moves a low wooden table out of our way. "Oh, no, my lovely. We have just begun."

Link

As the communication specialist of our trio, I am the host of the neuro-link we share and the one who first connected to our catalyst. Those two things mean that whether I'm present or not, I sense my brothers and our female having sex.

Not that I didn't already know.

Both Flash and Shift invited me to join their moment of intimacy with Lady Lark downstairs.

I declined and returned to my quarters.

It's not that I wouldn't like to explore the carnal pleasures of our bodies—mine and Lark's—of course, I would. But simply because she is the catalyst to the unlocking of our heightened abilities doesn't mean she is meant to be our lover.

Not that I can say that to Flash or Shift. No, the two of them are so eager to form a relationship and acknowledge the pull of our bonding, they don't want to question the alternatives or the repercussions.

Secluding myself into the private quarters I claimed when we arrived yesterday, I turn off the lights and lock the door. Lark and my brothers were making it difficult for me to focus on pool and conversation, so I thought it best that I turn in for the night.

The solitude makes it easier in some aspects and harder in others. Now my heightened state of arousal won't draw attention from young girls eager to ease our transition. Also, no one needs to ask me if I'm all right when my attention is lost in the sensations bombarding me.

With a grunt of frustration, I flop onto the bed and fight the urge to go downstairs to find them.

I feel their bonds tightening—to one another—but not to me.

Not that it bothers me.

Whenever Lark is near me, she is tentative and stiff. I never wanted to be tied to this mess, and she knows it. Whether it's the power of the universe or biology or something in the design of our creation, the reaction we're having to one another is still a choice.

My entire existence to this point has been determined by the preconceived notions of others. I refuse to tie my future to a female simply because there was a chemical reaction between us.

I am more than my programming.

Besides, if I could choose a female to pair with, she would be a complement to me. She would be submissive and yield to my logic. She would be soft and subdued, not challenging.

Lark is strong and beautiful, but she thinks herself our equal. Does she not understand we were designed and created to be superior to her kind?

The magic of the universe bound us—that's fine.

That bond doesn't mean she is meant to be mine.

A wave of lust pulses through Shift's interface and I grind my teeth to ride it out. My cock has been stone stiff for days. The only relief I've felt was when I pleasured myself, watching Flash and Lark join that first time in the bunker.

Images from that moment drift back and I hear the creak of the wooden table as Flash pinned Lark beneath him, the soft *click, click, click* of my juices being slicked over the tip of my erection as my palm squeezed and my arm pumped hard and fast.

After unfastening my waistband, I lift my hips and shove my pants down the bed. I may not want to be tied to the sexual bonding my brothers are so eager for, but I'm still a male.

And no one need know I'm riding their arousal.

Naked and splayed on the top of my bed, I spread my thighs and glare up at the ceiling.

This isn't about Lark.

This is basic biology.

I swipe a hand over my pecs and twist the knotted bud of my nipple. A sharp tingle prickles my nerve endings and my already stiff cock jumps against my abs. I reach low, gripping my testicles in my free hand, and open the neuro-link to the others.

I'm in their heads, living their thoughts in real time, and if I'm doing this right, they won't know I'm there with them.

Closing my eyes, I call my palm higher, gripping the problem at hand. The moment my fingers tighten around my length, my hips convulse. Damn. It feels like my balls are so tight they might explode from the built up pressure.

Somewhere over the past week, the urge to join with Lark has increased beyond an annoying ache and is now a full-on need.

I need this.

I need her.

But I don't.

I squeeze my shaft and the pressure is electric. A moan rumbles out of my chest as my erection kicks in my hand.

Shift feels so good.

The pleasure driving him fills me and I sink into the sensation, striking an aggressive rhythm. This isn't me giving in to the need of accepting Lark.

This is basic, physical biology.

I arch my shoulders as I continue to pleasure myself. Erotic images of Lark invade my moment. I try to block Shift's ocular input, but the scene in my head isn't coming from him.

These are *my* memories.

This is from when I watched Flash pumping into Lark in the bunker. My fingers dig into the covers, the fabric tearing beneath the force of my grip.

My breath tightens in my chest and I use my heightened abilities to pick up speed. *It's... so good.*

The feminine sounds Lark made as her pleasure built. The intoxicating scent of her core weeping for my brother's attention...

The need to release burns hot inside me. I open the neuro-link wider, letting all the input from Shift and Flash flood my receptors.

Oh... Faster. Harder.

I brace my free hand against the wall above my head and dig my heels into the mattress. With my breathing coming in panted breaths, I thrust my hips into the air and arc off the bed.

I'm about to explode.

Yes! Oh, yes, Shift.

Lark's insides clench on Shift's cock and squeeze him in a pulsing grip. Shift's mental energy fritzes, his cognitive system getting knocked off-line. Lark cries out, again shouting as Shift's entire body ignites with a violent release.

I throw my head back, suspended at the edge of the most glorious pleasure, my entire body tight with hunger. I'm on fire, quivering with the need to let loose. When Shift hits his climax... so do I.

"Yes!" I hammer at myself with a pounding rhythm, my release bursting to freedom. *"Yes."*

Streams of hot cream spurt free from my cock as I stroke and pant and never want the feeling to end. Strained grunts tear from behind my clenched jaw, my heaving chest and aching arms splattered with the reward of my hard work.

Sagging back to the surface of the bed, I slow my rhythm and ride out the last of my release. My systems are having trouble recalibrating, and if I'm not mistaken, I may have just masturbated myself through a coronary.

The glow of the moons highlights the carnal cum painting I've ejaculated all over myself and my bed.

I'm a genuine artist.

I am so creative.

Laying there in the near darkness, I breathe deeply until the world stops spinning and my skin chills from the sweat and cum. I consider getting up, getting dressed, and making my way to the bathroom to clean up... but then I feel Shift and Flash getting aroused again.

Damn, this might be a very long night.

CHAPTER ELEVEN

Mac

With only two days before the Amberloq hopefuls arrive to take part in the trials, there is no time to delay with Lark's training. Yes, she fought like a wildcat against the Gen-3 soldiers in the bunker, but the truth is, she was ill-prepared for an opponent like that and she suffered serious injuries.

If she'd been with anyone other than Shift and Lukas, she likely would have died.

Even thinking about that makes me woozy. What would've happened then? The three wouldn't have anyone to champion their needs and wants. Dornte wouldn't have a Biome General for the Forested Jungle. And I wouldn't have anyone who truly understands what it's like to be bound to men like the three.

The only way to safeguard against losing her is to work on her training and get her skills polished enough that we lower the risk of having her taken from us.

It's not like she doesn't have skills—she does.

She's fast and she's defensively very strong with her wings.

She's also determined to prove herself almost to the point of it being dangerous.

One of the first things I teach the soldiers in my squads is that with injuries, they need to be honest with themselves and the other members of the team. It does no one any good to have a member of the team secretly bleeding internally and refusing treatments when caught in the thick of things.

Although there was no 'good time' for her to collapse, having her succumb to her injuries after the battle was better than if we'd still been fighting full-tilt in the bunker.

Dropping out of the sky was less than ideal.

"Hold!" I call a stop to the maneuver and Flash and Lark stop sparring. We've done this enough times now that they know to freeze in place so Tundra or I can move in and explain where Lark went off course.

It's me who spotted her misstep this time, and it's important enough that I want to ensure we correct it before she develops any bad habits.

Moving into their circle, I step in behind Lark. "When Flash came at ye with the overhand strike to yer weak side, ye pivoted yer hips to angle yer block to intercept his blade. That not only twisted yer stance, but it kept ye within strikin' range. Instead, try this."

I move in tight to her ass and wrap an arm around her waist. "Move with me, little bird. Flash, rewind that last attack and reenact it in slow motion, if ye will."

Flash cants his head to the side like a curious pup and then resets his position. I angle Lark back to the starting standoff and get ready to show her where she went wrong. "When he comes at ye like that, yer first instinct is to meet his attack, but if ye slide yer left leg back, the movement will naturally twist yer body so yer dominant side angles to block his strike and yer stance hasn't been compromised."

I move her the first time so she gets the feel of the motion

I'm describing and then set her back into the starting position again. "All right, Flash. From the beginning."

We move through the adjustment once more and she smiles over her shoulder at me. "Yeah, I feel that. It widens a defensive stance instead of twisting me up."

"Aye, and keeps ye from bein' knocked over if the strike connects." I release my hold on her and back away. "And again."

Tundra and I watch them resume their sparring match and I smile when she makes the adjustment and blocks Flash's downward strike without issue. "That's right, lass. Ye got it."

Tundra grins and leans closer. "She picks things up quickly."

"Aye, she does at that. She's got a natural grace and awareness of self that can't be learned. It'll help her become the fighter she'll need to be soon enough."

Tundra nods. "Thank you for offering your perspective. I think it's important, especially with the Gen-3 soldiers being programmed and conditioned in the Amberloq fighting styles, that we learn other defensive and offensive tactics."

"Agreed. It certainly can't hurt." I watch for a few more minutes and then Lark launches forward with a closed fist. "Hold."

Lark

WHEN MAC CALLS for us to hold, I swallow and catch my breath. My muscles are quivering, my wings are aching, and there is sweat running down my butt crack and pooling under my boobs.

"Flash, give us the floor fer a moment, lad. I want to work with yer lady a little face-to-face."

Flash bows his head and steps back with a wink. *Kiss his butt, my lovely.*

I bust up laughing. *You mean kick his butt, sweetie. Very different.*

Mac moves to stand in front of me and shakes out his shoulders. I watch as the toned muscles of his arms swing loose and his hands fall free to his sides. I expect him to take some sort of fighting stance, but he doesn't. He looks relaxed.

"Now, attack me like ye just did Flash."

I watch him for a few racing heartbeats and shake out my nerves. I've grown comfortable sparring against Flash and know he doesn't judge my shortcomings as a fighter. I'm not there with Mac.

Not that I think he'll judge me...

And not that I mind when he uses his hands-on approach to train me...

"Have ye run out of steam, then?" he asks.

Right. I size him up and circle, looking for my opening. He's about the same height as me, the two of us a good six inches shorter than the three. But smaller doesn't equate to him being weaker, because he's pinned me half a dozen times this evening already. I study his expression, trying to read him, but his playful, hazel gaze gives nothing away.

"We don't have all night, lass," he teases.

I scramble forward, fists up to block, and swing my wing around from the right. My attack doesn't catch him off-guard in the slightest. The moment I launch into action, he drops into a fighting stance and is ready for me.

He ducks the swing of my wing and grabs the spine, swinging me around. My head spins as I'm twirled away from him and he steps in close to my back again. "Nice try, little bird," he whispers next to my ear.

His breath is warm against the hairs on the side of my neck and I shiver.

Too soon, he releases me and spins me to face him again. "That's why I stopped yer attack on Flash. Ye telegraph yer intentions. Lookin' where yer about to attack makes it blatantly obvious to yer opponent what they can expect. Now, go again."

I shake off the momentary distraction of him being too cocky and cute and settle back into the moment. This time, when I come at him, I make a concerted effort not to give my intentions away.

I pretend I'm going to punch with my right and then sweep fast with my left foot. The arch of my boot narrowly misses catching his calf as he leaps into the air and staggers back a couple of steps to regain his footing.

"Och, much better, ye wee sneak. Much better indeed."

A small swell of pride bursts free in my chest.

"Again, little bird. See if ye can dance with the cat and come out of it with all yer feathers." He waggles his brows at me.

So cocky.

But not in a bad way.

Where Link is cocky and arrogant, his high opinion of himself comes from him truly believing the hype that they built him to be superior to everyone else. With Mac, his teasing confidence comes from having a firm base of knowledge and experience but still acknowledging that others could not only surprise him, but beat him in a fight.

I think he actually wants me to beat him.

Challenge accepted.

"How are you so fast?" I ask after a few more times of me trying to catch him unaware.

"I use my shifter senses to add to my human abilities. Ye need to do the same. Unless yer facin' off against other Elbirfae, ye'll always have a distinct set of physical attributes than yer opponent. Look fer ways to use those differences to yer advantage."

I think about that as we circle again, studying his physical attributes to determine how I should counter them with mine.

Rolling my shoulders, I flush. His physical attributes are too distracting. If I want to learn how to be a better fighter, I need to 'not' study them.

For the next hour, we dance this dance. Mac pits me against Flash, then challenges me himself, and by the end of the evening, he partners me with Tundra and the two of us go up against the two of them.

When I trip over nothing for the second time, Mac calls it a night. "Ye did well, lass. It's best to end things on a win. Yer feet are gettin' sloppy, and I don't want ye back in the medical bay."

Flash settles in beside me and wraps an arm around the small of my back. "No. We don't want that."

Mac looks around at Tundra. "Tell me there's a steam room or a hot tub or somethin' somewhere in this mansion."

Tundra nods. "We have both. Lower level, east wing, just off the weight room."

Mac nods. "Excellent. Come, lass, let's go do a proper cool down and then treat yer muscles to a little luxury. After a workout like that, we'll need to end things properly or we're likely to stiffen."

At the mention of him stiffening, my libido kicks in and yeah, Mac standing there all sweaty and toned doesn't help.

The embarrassing part is that the moment he breathes in, his brow arches and the corner of his mouth quirks up.

Stupid shifter sense of smell.

"I'll leave you to your evening then," Tundra says.

I'm not sure if he's aware of how my female desires have gotten away from me, but if he is, he doesn't let on. Tundra's good like that. He's warm and friendly, but he's also professional and private. If it was Dune, he'd be whistling and catcalling as we leave. Thankfully, Dune and Lukas are busy working with the kids tonight.

"Thank you for your help," I say, picking up a towel and patting my face and chest. "Have a good night."

As Tundra finishes his goodbyes and heads back inside, I

turn my back on Flash and Mac, shoving the towel under my shirt to mop up some of the less feminine sweaty areas. Well, I suppose breasts are very feminine... but what's happening there isn't.

"Shall we?" Mac says, gesturing toward the doors to the lower level.

They are the same doors I came out the other night when I was looking for Mac after he blew up at Shift. The same doors I used to go back inside to find Flash waiting to take me...

An erotic mental replay of our threesome in the rec room springs to mind and another wild rush of wanton hits. Being pinned by Shift against the fireplace. Being laid out over the coffee table as Flash joined us...

"Ye either need to tamp down yer inner vixen or head somewhere private, lass, because I'm strong... but my cat has limits. Keep it up and I'll have yer legs spread and be lickin' at that cream before ye know it."

I gasp at the growl lining his words and meet his gaze. Mac's hazel eyes usually dance with a level of teasing...

Right now, they aren't dancing—they're smoldering.

I swallow and bite my lip. "Sorry. It's, uh, my hormones have run a little wild on me lately."

"Likely all that cock ye've been gettin'."

There's no judgment or censure in the growl of his voice, but I can't quite read his emotions. Does it bother him that Shift has been joining Flash and me at night? And if so... is it because he wants to be with Shift, or me, or maybe both?

The boys regularly talk about the pull they feel toward me and Shift toward Mac. I admit, when I look at our Scottish Sith, I feel a pull there too.

But before I can dig myself too deep into that hole, Mac clears his throat. "Och, on second thought. I forgot I need to check on somethin'. Flash, if ye will, take yer lady to the steam room and give her a wee rub down to soothe her aches."

"You're not coming?" I ask, my voice sounding a little too disappointed, even to my own ears.

"No. I have things to finish up, but will catch up with ye in the morning."

As he strides away, I check out his fine ass and laugh at my disappointment.

I'm becoming a very greedy girl.

I've begun collecting lovers like butterflies.

CHAPTER TWELVE

Flash

*A*fter twenty minutes in the steam room and massaging Lark's muscles until they are once again supple to my touch, we change back into our clothes and I scoop her into my arms. She's almost boneless as I carry her up the stairs back to our room. She's exhausted. The moment I begin walking, her head lolls against my chest and her eyes fall closed.

That's it, beautiful. I've got you.

She's truly worn herself out.

Between late nights of sexual play with Shift and me, and training hard with Mac, Lukas, Tundra, and Dune, she has been going hard for days.

And I couldn't be prouder of her.

When I get back to our suite, I open my mental connection with my brothers and Link responds by opening the door. He glances at Lark, asleep in my arms, and his brow tightens. *Is she ill?*

No. She's tired. I take her straight inside, tuck her into our bed for some much-needed rest, and close the door behind me as I join Link in the living room. *She has been training for hours each day and night and used up her energy store completely.*

It doesn't matter how much she trains, she will never exceed the maximum abilities of an Elbirfae female. Our enemies will still be stronger.

My mouth falls open. *Why must you be such a superior ass? Her fighting skills have improved. You should praise her growth, not condemn her for not being created with our specifications.*

No. You shouldn't encourage her to think herself equal to our enemies in a fight. You're going to get her killed.

I laugh. *Don't pretend you care about her well-being.*

Don't presume to know my feelings.

I meet the challenge of his glare and shake my head. *Feelings? Please. Your haughty disdain hangs around us all like a foul smell.*

And your lack of self-esteem is embarrassing. She's a female, Flash. There are another three-hundred thousand of them in the quadrant just like her.

No, there aren't. Lark is unique and loyal, loving and spectacular.

And you follow her around like a pup in heat.

Fuck you!

Listen to yourself, you even talk like them now.

Because I'm learning and evolving. You're still as stiff and selfish as you've always been.

Selfish? Everything I do is for you, Shift, Alpha, and Beta. Do you think I enjoy standing as the sole voice of reason? To be the one on the outside?

Yes, I do. I think you put yourself up on a dais and can't understand why no one wants to worship you. You're right where you want to be. You simply want us to be there with you like we always were.

He grabs my shirt with both hands and slams me into the wall. *You ungrateful child. After everything I've done for you —*

I swing my leg and bring my knee up, connecting with his ribs. He lets out a grunt, and I pull myself free. *What you've done for me? You mean making all my decisions and implying I'm not as good as you —*

—You're not! You're emotional, you trust too easily, and you cannot see the dangers closing in on you. It's a shortcoming that puts you in danger and, in turn, puts all of us in danger.

No. Even before my heightened abilities activated, I could read people better than you. I trust those who deserve it. Not everyone is our enemy.

And not everyone is our friend.

Lark is our friend.

He laughs. *No, Flash. I am your friend. Shift is your friend. Alpha and Beta are your friends. We are the people who deserve your trust and yet you've only got eyes for the female who opens her knees for you.*

My fist flies and connects with the side of his face with the force of an anvil. His head is knocked sideways and his optical systems flicker as they recalibrate. *Say what you will about me, but if you utter another unflattering word about Lark, I will forget we're friends altogether.*

The door swings opens and Shift rushes inside. *Stop this. The two of you are giving me a headache.*

The two of us look at our brother and it takes a moment for the haze of fury to clear.

"Are our emotions bleeding through the mental connection?" Link asks.

Shift runs his fingers through his hair and scowls. "How could they not? The two of you are shouting so loud over our mental channel, I could hear you across the compound."

Link frowns. "I never meant…"

"Your emotions must have shorted out your control," Shift says, stepping between us.

Link probes the mottled skin of his face where I hit him. "I didn't realize."

"Clearly." Lark's voice is hard and when I turn to see her

standing in the doorway of our bedroom, her scowl is even harder. "And if Shift got a headful across the compound, you can imagine what I got lying in the next room."

I throw Link a dirty look and stride toward her. "Pay no attention to him, my lovely. He didn't mean it. Things got heated, and he spoke out of anger."

Her green gaze meets mine, and her expression softens. "I heard what he said, and I felt the emotions behind his words. There's no need to protect my feelings. He meant every word."

Link has the decency to look remorseful. "Lady Lark... Flash is right. I spoke out of anger."

"Then let me return the favor. Get the slecking hell out of this suite." She holds out her arm and points toward the door. "There are enough rooms in this compound for you to get far away from me. I'm done sticking up for you. I'm done trying to make you feel welcome. I'm just done."

Link steps forward, pressing a hand to his chest. "Lark, truly, I apologize. I shouldn't have said—"

"—No, you shouldn't. Now leave."

As angry as I am at my brother—and I *am* angry—I also feel bad for my part in this situation. "My lovely..."

She shakes her head. "No, Flash. I realize it's been the three of you against the world for decades, but I won't have him in my space cutting me down when I've done nothing to deserve it. Besides, it's not like he cares. I'm just a female like any other, only he can be damned sure I won't be opening my knees for him."

And with that, she steps back into the bedroom and slams the door.

Link

THE PAIN and fury that flashes in Lark's green gaze as she throws me out of our suite is both stunning and disheartening. She has fire, that's for sure.

I wander the halls of the retreat mansion and run through the recordings of my fight with Flash. I said nothing that wasn't true, and yet they have made me out to be a villain.

Fact: Lark *isn't* as strong or capable as our enemies.

Fact: False encouragement *could* get her killed.

Fact: There are hundreds of thousands of females in the quadrant that could offer sexual distraction.

Although, it's true what he said too. Lark *is* unique because she has been loyal to us.

Until now.

"Hey, Link. Did you come down for a game?" The young girl's words draw my attention to the teen Elbirfae, Skye, looking at me from inside the room with the pool table. She's passing her time with Dune and her boyfriend, Yarko, the boy who can portal.

"Another time, perhaps. I don't think I would be good company tonight. It seems I am selfish and speak without considering the ramifications of my opinions."

Dune barks a laugh and straightens at the table. "Then you *definitely* should join us because no one here knows more about that personality flaw than me."

He glances back down to finish lining up his shot and then strikes the cue ball. The white sphere is propelled across the table, clacking and cracking into the other balls. The ricochet of the chaos knocks a striped green ball into the corner pocket. When the table falls still, he hands Skye his cue and tells her to take his place.

Then, he waves me in and heads over to the bar on the far wall.

My first instinct is to refuse his offer of camaraderie, but then I remember Flash's admonishment that he has been learning and evolving while I have remained stiff and arrogant.

Fine. If only to prove him wrong, I will engage with these people.

Since Dune has taken up position behind the bar, I select one of the stools and claim a seat.

"What will you have?"

"Haze with ice."

The Elbirfae passes me a stout glass and sets one on his side of the bar for himself. After selecting a bottle of rich burgundy liquid from the shelf, he makes a liberal pour for both of us and then offers his glass up to clink. The ritual is not lost on me. As more and more of my secondary programming comes online, I find fewer things confuse me.

"So, you spouted off and pissed people off. Tell me. What was that about?"

I take a sip of the alcohol and admire its potency. By my chemical analysis, at this size, eight glasses of this libation will render me intoxicated. Perhaps Flash is right and I've been neglecting my experiences in the realm.

"Seriously, Link. You don't know me well, but I've got you. There isn't anything you could've said or done to the people around you that would shock me."

"It's been brought to my attention recently that I lack the skill to treat others as my equals."

Dune nods. "Why do you think that is? You, Flash, and Shift were all created to the same specifications, and yet they are friendly and personable."

"I believe it's because I find it difficult to see the value of wasting my time and talents on those inferior to me."

Dune takes a long swallow of his drink and chuckles. "And who falls into the category of being inferior to you?"

I consider that. "Everyone."

"That's what I thought you were going to say."

"Because it is the truth."

He tops up our glasses and shrugs. "Maybe in some ways, but let me ask you this. For all the programming you have and the physical abilities you possess, do you know everything?"

"No. Of course not."

"Right, so, the other night, who taught you how to play pool?"

I glance over at the young couple flirting and playing pool. "Skye did."

"And do you consider her inferior to you?"

"Yes."

"Why?"

"Because she is a child. She does not possess the strength or intelligence to best me, therefore, I am better."

He arches a brow. "All right. I'll agree she doesn't have the physical strength of you or your brothers, but that doesn't mean she's not strong. That girl watched goblin soldiers murder her parents and her siblings. She was kidnapped from her home, beaten and abused by goblins for two years, and yet she still finds the courage every day to get up, be kind to the people she meets, and offer them what comfort and knowledge she has."

I consider his assessment, but fail to see how that negates my point.

"Do you believe she has a strength of character and will to survive those things and still be a warm and caring young female?"

"Yes, I suppose so."

"And did she teach you—a male who is intellectually superior to her—how to play a parlor game and enjoy an evening of social interaction?"

"She did."

"So, she's not smarter than you, but she has knowledge and skills in areas you don't. Her world experiences have been different, as have yours. And even though she won't ever be a super soldier, she has things to both offer you and teach you."

I watch the way the girl bounces around the table. Her smile is open and infectious and having received her kindness the other night with Alpha and Beta, I agree, her fondness is freely given.

Dune takes another drink and waits until my attention returns to him. "There is no better or worse, inferior or superior. Everyone you come across will have strengths and knowledge and things to offer. If you only value that based on what you deem important in a battle, then you miss out on what those people could offer you in life."

I honestly hadn't thought about it that way. "And that's what my brothers have been doing?"

"From where I'm standing, yes. They've been taking the time to get to know all of us and to find out what it means to build friendships and relationships."

"Flash is overly infatuated with Lark. I pointed out to him she is a female like any other and simply because she takes him into her bed, does not make her our equal."

"Ouch. You really did spout off."

"And Lark overheard."

Dune's sandy blond eyebrows arch, and he points to my face. "And he slugged you in the face?"

"Yes. Though, I stand by what I said. She is a female he just met. I have been his brother through our entire existence, yet he chooses her over me."

"He's falling in love with her. You can't look at the two of them and not see that."

I grunt and finish my drink. "Love isn't part of our programming. We are soldiers. Building a relationship with our catalyst is unnecessary. She has already unlocked our heightened abilities."

Dune chuckles and refills my glass. "I can guarantee you,

when Flash is with Lark, he's not looking at her and seeing your catalyst."

"Then what is it?"

He blinks at me and then snaps his fingers in front of my eyes. "Hello? Are these things working?"

I ease back. "I assure you, my ocular system is functioning at full specification."

"Then you should realize that Lark is exceptional. She's beautiful and strong and dedicated. She's protective and caring and she'll put herself between someone she cares about and certain death without a second thought."

"Which is illogical."

"No, it's brave. Despite losing everything during the raids of the Usurper Queen, she rose to the challenge of leading and protecting the captives of that goblin camp. She stands up for people who need her and she does that because she cares."

I take a long drink, liking the way my extremities are getting a little numb and tingly. "But we have never needed her protection. We are super soldiers."

He shakes his head. "You have to be the dumbest smart person I've ever met."

"Why do you say that?"

"You are only where you are because Lark stood up for you. Who do you think argued to keep you out of stasis? Who offered to move in with you when protocol dictated you three be under lock and guard? Who do you think convinced us that the super soldier program may have been a mistake but that the three—or five—of you weren't?"

It's nothing I didn't know already, but hearing him say it like that makes me realize perhaps I owe Lark more loyalty than I've given her. "I stand by my assessment that she does not have the strength or skill in battle that we do."

"And no one is trying to say she does… but she has so much you and your brothers don't. So does Lukas. So does Mac. I would take a tactical team like our group over a programmed super soldier team any day of the week because dude—you don't know what you don't know."

"Obviously, but—"

"No buts. Our diversity and differing levels of training, strength, and experience make us better. You sold Lark short and insulted not only her, but everything she's done for the three of you. That's why Flash punched you in the face."

I touch the contusion on my cheek and tilt my shoulders to look at the bruising in my mirrored reflection behind the bar. "And because of all these things, I am *not* superior to her or the rest of you."

"Now you're catching on."

"But I am."

"In some ways, but also not."

That is a great deal of information to consider. "Do you mind if I take this? I wish to find a quiet place and process the things you've said."

Dune gestures to the bottle. "Have at it. And Link?"

I rise from my stool and meet his gaze as I grip the neck of the bottle. "Yes?"

"You fucked up with Lark. Your brothers will probably accept an apology, but you'll owe her something more."

"What kind of more?"

He lifts a shoulder. "An expression of your remorse, a grand gesture, a sacrifice to prove to her you've learned something and you realize how stupid you've been."

I frown. "You think I've been stupid? With my programming, I don't even think that is possible."

He chuckles and upends his glass, swallowing the last of his drink. "Oh, it's possible. Trust me."

CHAPTER THIRTEEN

Shift

Lark's resiliency never ceases to amaze me. Even after Link insulted her and made her cry, she woke up, invited Alpha and Beta into our suite for breakfast, and is teaching them the basic cooking skills she taught us last week when we first stayed in the bunker with her.

In her words, "It doesn't matter how many attackers you can kill—if you can't feed yourself, you can't fuel yourself."

"Everything smells wonderful," Tundra says, joining us in the kitchen downstairs. "I'm sorry you had to trouble yourselves."

"Nonsense," Lark says, demonstrating how to slide the spatula underneath a pancake to flip it. "We made sure to get down here before you so that we could feed you for a change."

"And learn how to fuel ourselves," Beta says, smiling. "We're making pancakes."

Tundra pours himself a cup of coffee. "Lark is a smart lady. Fighting on an empty stomach is never advisable."

I stand when he comes to the table. "Take my seat. I'm off to meet Lukas in the cell area downstairs."

Tundra nods. "Do you know where you're going?"

"He said it was at the back of the west wing and I was to enter from outside."

Tundra sets his mug down and heads back to the counter to collect a plate of food. "That's right. You'll have no trouble finding it."

I stride over to kiss Lark's cheek and rinse my plate before leaving. "Be well, beautiful."

She winks at me. "Enjoy your interrogation."

I will. At least, I hope I will.

Link will also be involved with this interrogation and I'm not sure what kind of mood he will be in after last night.

I leave them to their morning and strike off through the vast corridors, heading to the back doors.

As my feet beat out a steady rhythm, I can't help but wonder where our brother ended up after Lark sent him away.

Yes, he deserved Lark's ire and no, I don't forgive him for hurting her when she's done nothing but be kind to us, but like Flash... I see in Link what most people don't.

He acts tough, and he talks gruff, but of the three of us, he's actually the one most afraid of being cast aside. And so, he pushes at people and lashes out until that's exactly what happens.

Pushing through the glass door, I stare up at the new day. The mountains are breathtaking.

Removing my shirt, I release my wings and fly over the building to the west wing. Yes, I could've walked and absorbed the scenery a little longer, but honestly, I am eager to meet up with Link and Lukas and find out what we can from the Gen-3 soldiers we captured back at the bunker.

The air is crisp from the altitude and I wonder how that will affect our performance in the days to come. There's no actual qualifying for us to be part of the Amberloq squads, but Lukas and the Biome Generals all agree that it is in our best interest to go through the training with everyone else, if only to learn what everyone else will learn.

My boots touch down on the stone pathway, and I reach for the door. As it swings out at me, I step back and let Mac exit.

He seems as startled to see me as I am to see him. "Och, sorry about that."

I shrug. "No harm done."

He looks me up and down and I realize I still have my shirt in my hand. "Apologies."

Releasing my wings, I pull my shirt over my head and tug the bottom hem down.

He's still staring.

I take another step back, unsure if I'm still too close for his liking.

He doesn't move.

"Have I done something else to upset you?"

"Och, no. I'm not upset. Ye just caught me off-guard, that's all."

I take another step back. Surely if he wants to leave, he has room enough. "I assure you, I didn't know you would be here, and I have done nothing but stay away."

His expression falls.

"I don't know what else I can do to keep you from hating me."

He blinks. "I don't hate ye. What would ever give ye the impression I did?"

"You avoid me. You get angry whenever you're around me. And the last time we spoke, you made it very clear you want nothing to do with the bonding attraction drawing us into each other's lives."

He steps forward and I step back to ensure he has the space he needs. When he continues to advance, I step back against the wall. Unable to retreat any further, I hold my palms up, unsure of what to do next.

Mac curses. "Are ye really that afraid of me, lad?"

"Afraid of you? No. Afraid to anger you and alienate you even further? Yes, definitely."

He exhales and shakes his head, his deep russet waves brushing his shoulder. "I'm sorry. I've handled this whole situation wrong from the beginning, and made ye feel like it's yer fault. It's not."

My heart is beating fast in my chest. "What are you saying?"

He lifts the corner of his mouth in a crooked smile as he leans even closer. "I'm sayin' that ignorin' the pull and keepin' my distance hasn't done me a damned bit of good. If the universe wants us together, it's not takin' no fer an answer."

My mind is spinning, running through the combinations and permutations of possible meanings for his comment.

They all come back with the same outcome...

"Are you saying—"

His lips claim mine in a move so quick I don't even have time to think, let alone react.

So much for super soldier reaction time.

His mouth moves over mine with the same eagerness we shared during our first kiss in the forest. Only, this time, there isn't the same edge of hostility. It might be too much to hope for, and maybe I'm projecting, but it feels like he actually *wants* to kiss me.

Fine by me.

He can have me in whatever capacity he wants.

And though it's only been a couple of days since he yelled at me and dropped out of my life, it feels like it has been much longer. I missed this closeness.

I missed *him*.

His palms claim both sides of my jaw, his fingers digging into the flesh as if he can't pull me close enough. When he breaks from our kiss, he's panting and breathless. "Feckin' hell, yer addictive."

"And that's a good thing?"

"Aye, I meant it that way."

Oh, good. Then I will stand as the object of his addiction. In fact, I couldn't be happier.

Not wanting the moment to slip away, I move my hands to his hips and pull him closer, taking his lips with mine once again.

A lot has changed since our 'frenzied fuck in the forest', as he called it. Since then, my higher-level programs have activated, my social adaptations have taken hold, and I've spent every free moment pleasuring Lark and learning the nuances of intimacy.

What we shared the first time was new and a shock to me. This time, I can hold my own.

When he eases back, the gold highlights in his eyes are twinkling like stars glimmering in the night sky. "Ye've been practicin'."

Heat warms my cheeks. "That doesn't anger you?"

"Och, no. Ye made yer intentions clear the other morning when we talked about expectations. I'm well aware of the fact that things have progressed with yer relationship with Lark."

"Lark is a giving and beautiful female."

"I'm sure she is."

I swallow. "I, uh, I'm not sure what any of this means."

Mac chuckles. "That's fine. Neither do I."

"But you're not angry that we kissed? You don't regret it like you did the last time?"

He exhales a heavy breath. "No. I don't regret it. And if the truth be told, I didn't regret it the last time either. That's what made me angriest of all. What we did in that forest was passionate and wild, but exactly what I needed at that moment."

"And what about this moment?"

His mouth curls up in that crooked smile of his. "Weel, I think Link and Lukas are waitin' on ye, so we'll have to table this discussion until yer done in there. If ye like... when yer finished, come knock on the door to my quarters and maybe we could spend some private time figurin' a few things out?"

I fight to find my voice. "Yes. I would like that."

Link

AT LONG LAST, Shift arrives at the cell area and we can begin our interrogation. Despite my assuring Lukas that I can infiltrate the thoughts and memories of the captured soldiers without causing damage to the integrity of their minds, he insisted that Shift be present in case they need to be healed.

His lack of confidence is noted.

It's also unwarranted.

I spent a great deal of time last night considering Dune's words of counsel and while I see the wisdom in much of what he had to say, I also stand by my belief that there are situations where I *am* superior.

And with my heightened abilities as a communications specialist gifted in neuro-interface, voice analysis, and negotiations, there is no one better suited for this task than me.

"Good morning, Shift," Lukas says, extending a hand in welcome as he joins us.

"Good morning to you both."

I give him a nod, unsure where the two of us stand after last night's altercation with Flash. If we were alone, I would ask him, but since we are not, and they brought us here with a job to do, I focus on the task at hand. "Shall we begin?"

Lukas gestures to the first door on the far wall. Beside it, there is a large viewing window with metal bars running vertically across the entire width. Through the space between the bars we can see beyond the security glass to where the female Gen-3 soldier is awaiting interrogation.

"We've kept them all sedated," Lukas says. "Our scientists back at the castle diluted the take-down serum and reformulated it for our purpose. They are awake but unable to launch an attack or access any of their heightened augments."

"What is your plan for them after interrogation?" Shift asks.

"They are the enemy," I say. "They should be decommissioned."

Lukas tilts his head from side to side. "Possibly, but that's not set in stone."

"But they attacked us!"

"And so did you," Lukas says, chuckling. "They were acting on a directive programmed into them by their maker. That doesn't necessarily make them our enemy. Perhaps they were simply misled and can be reasoned with."

Shift nods. "In which case, we could strengthen the Amberloq forces and enlist those captured to the true purpose of our creation."

"Unless Andras Brass programmed them with a different intention altogether," I say, pointing out what they are obviously overlooking. "He and his people had two years to not only develop their plan to divert the purpose of these soldiers, but also to form new alliances. How could we ever be truly certain of their allegiance?"

Lukas nods. "All good points, Link, and that's why we're here. We need to investigate all possibilities and determine whether these soldiers can be salvaged as part of this program or taken offline or imprisoned."

I know what I prefer, but my opinion is rooted in anger and distrust, so I keep it to myself. "Very well, let's begin."

CHAPTER FOURTEEN

Lark

After everyone is fed and the breakfast dishes are cleaned and put away, Alpha and Beta go off with Skye and Yarko and Flash and I are alone for the first time in hours.

He takes the dish towel from my hands and leads me away from the kitchen and down the wide hall toward the living areas. "What would you like to do for our last day before the applicants arrive and the trials of warrior selection begin?"

I think about that and smile. "How about a fly around the mountains and then a warm bath together to take the chill out of our bones?"

His expression lights up with an easy grin. "That sounds perfect. Let's go see if we can find any jackets in the supply closet. Dune said for us to help ourselves to anything we need."

The two of us change course and head toward the main foyer of the building.

"Speaking of the arrival of prospective warriors, how are you feeling about that?" I watch him closely to read if he's anxious about that.

"I'm looking forward to it, actually. Aside from the proceedings taking your time and attention away from me, I think it'll be good for both of us. You'll get to do more in your role as a Biome General and we'll meet new people and maybe learn some new fighting practices." He opens the door to the closet and the two of us go inside.

The closet is twenty feet deep and sloped at the ceiling where the stairs angle over us. Hanging rails full of jackets and gear hang down both sides, with boots and shoes lined up on the floor below. And on the back wall, floor-to-ceiling cubbies are filled with anything else we might need for all seasons.

After closing the door behind us, I inventory his body from head to toe and draw in a heavy breath. It would be so easy to abandon the idea of exploring the scenery outside and retreat to our suite upstairs.

But no... we are more than insatiable bodies.

Addressing the shelves, I select a few items for him to try on. I admit, I'm looking forward to the fashion show. Flash has an incredible body: broad, muscled shoulders, sculptured torso, slim waist.

The deep rumble of male amusement has me meeting his arched brow. "Are you certain you want to go flying?"

I swallow and hook a swath of hair behind my ear. "Yes, so stop distracting me with your sexiness."

He laughs. "My apologies."

I go back to moving jackets along the rod. Thankfully, until this point, all Amberloq have been Elbirfae, so the design of all these jackets takes my wings into account.

"What do you think about this one?"

I turn and burst out laughing as Flash holds up a yellow jacket covered in buckles. "I don't think so. You're not really a canary yellow kind of guy."

"But it might tamp down my sexiness so you can focus."

"It definitely would do that, but no, I have to learn to deal with your hotness and still function like I'm not about to melt into a heap of wet wanton."

He waggles his brow and steps forward, reaching for a jacket behind my shoulder. "What about this blue one? Do you think this would look good on me?"

Gods, he smells so good. I swallow, forcing my excitement down so my voice doesn't squeak. "I think you could wear anything and it would look good on you."

He smiles at my reaction, apparently liking how he affects me.

My hand strokes over the soft cotton of his shirt and I stare at the skin of his throat and chest below where the buttons hang open. He hums his approval and prowls closer.

I step back.

Grinning, he rests one hand on the coat rail above my head and sinks his fingers into my hair with the other.

I'm trapped within his frame.

He eyes me with the hungry focus of the predator he was. "Are you all right, my lovely? You seem a little flushed."

Our eyes lock in that 'touch my soul' way we sometimes share.

Motionless, I draw the scent of him deep into my lungs. I'm lost in the warmth of his whiskey golden eyes. I lick my lips, wondering if his heightened hearing can pick up the thundering rate of my pulse.

Flash's body presses hot against mine, the solid muscle of his frame accepted by my lush curves. Cupping my cheek, he leans in, taking a slow, deep breath along the length of my neck. I stifle a groan as his nose brushes my jaw. Warm breath tickles my neck, sending a shiver down my spine.

He touches his lips to mine, softly parting them as his tongue brushes the seam of my lips.

Everything about this is languid and patient.

The rapid hammering of his heart against my palm is the

only sign that he's not nearly as calm as he seems. I love the way he's holding me, gentle yet strained, and I know I'm not the only one fighting for control.

I meet his kiss and then, too soon, he pulls back, breathless. "Later. I'm looking forward to our bath... but if I'm to warm you up, first we must go out and get chilled."

"Or we could *not* get chilled and move straight to the good stuff."

He backs up, taking the blue jacket with him, and chuckles. "A reward is even more satisfying after earning it. Come, let's go explore the mountain peaks."

Mac

I GRAB my t-shirt off the end of the bed and toss it into a drawer, then move my boots from the center of the floor to sit neatly beside the door. Straightening up, I cast a surveying glance around my quarters and then laugh at myself.

Why am I nervous about making a good impression? Shift is a sure thing. There's no doubt the two of us want to get naked and figure out what's driving us together... but there's something else happening, too.

It's that other part of the equation I missed at first.

My cat didn't.

My Sith side runs more intensely on instinct than I do as a man and my cat wants to curl up in Shift's lap and let off a long, throaty purr.

That's an entirely unfamiliar sensation for me.

Not that I haven't had dozens of lovers—both male and female—I have. What's new is that my cat is weighing in on me getting together with Shift. My animal side might've gotten worked up and wanted to let loose with a lover, but it's about pleasure and often the release of stress.

With Shift, it's different.

With Shift, my cat is pacing and possessive. It's more than just pleasure and releases he seeks. It's the potential of claiming a mate. The moment I realized that was when I knew whatever plans the universe has, they won't be undone by me simply being stubborn and tossing off in cold showers until this passes.

This is happening.

Whatever 'this' is... yeah, it's happening.

I glance around the room for the last look and am pleased with the work of the past hour. We've got a nice snack spread set out. The room is warm enough to spend time without clothes on, and with the lamps I found when raiding the other rooms, we can have light without the harsh brilliance of the ceiling fixture.

And if the afternoon takes us where I'm hoping it will, I've got candles and bath salts and scented massage oils too.

The knock on my door isn't the strong alert that a super soldier has arrived. It's the unsure question of whether or not this is really happening.

It is.

I open the door and step back, gesturing for him to join me. When he strides inside, I lock the door so we won't be interrupted. "How were the interrogations?"

"I believe Lukas was pleased. Between the four prisoners, Link got addresses of places they stayed and a list of names of people Andras Brass has spoken to."

"Good, good. I'm sure Lukas will be pleased with that. He'll have Rhylan track those leads down and we can get Alpha Squad ready to move out as soon as he does."

He shoves his hands in his pockets as he studies the room. "I'm sure your squad will be glad to have you back."

"Aye, I'm sure. Warriors never like too much downtime. They like to keep busy, to keep their blades sharp."

Why are we talking about this? Right. Because I suck at small talk.

"Would ye like to sit and have a bite to eat? Are ye hungry?"

He looks at the food and then forces a smile. "Of course. Thank you for this. Everything looks wonderful."

I chuckle. "Now I know yer just bein' polite."

His smile falls. "No. Really. I appreciate your efforts... and your invitation to figure things out."

I hold out my hands and he doesn't hesitate to give me his palms. "Yer hands are shakin'."

"Yes, my motor-stabilization system seems to be malfunctioning. Apologies."

Damn. Why do I think it's so adorable when he says shit like that? I really am a goner. "Ye don't need to apologize. Come here and sit."

I lead him over to the end of the bed and sit him down. "Relax. I'm not goin' to lose my temper or yell at ye or make ye feel bad about what we feel fer one another. That's over. Do ye understand?"

He nods and looks at where I'm still holding his hand. "What changed?"

Kneeling before him, I undo his boots and ease his feet free, one at a time. When they're both set on the floor, I crawl onto the bed and invite him to lie on his side facing me. "I realized I was being a coward. Both Lukas and Hawk, two of my closest friends, have been bound to their mates and once they got out of their way, wondrous things happened. I suppose I'm just a little thick in the skull. It took me a bit to accept that."

With his head on the opposite pillow and our bodies close enough to touch, he seems to settle down a little. "But you accept it now?"

I gather his hand in mine and snuggle forward a little more, so there's less than a foot between us. "I accept we've been given an opportunity for happiness and the universe wants us together for whatever reason, but it's still our decision on how we handle things."

He bites his bottom lip, his gaze studying me. "And how do you wish to handle things?"

"I thought I should start by treatin' ye better than I have, and maybe let ye be on the receivin' end of my apology."

I regret the wounds I caused with my rejection. None of this was his fault, and I had no right to take my frustration out on him and make him feel like it was. He deserves more from me than a mere apology.

"Shift, do ye trust me?"

"I think so," he says, reading my expression. "I want to."

Oh, my heart. The fact that he's unsure cleaves me in two. "I deserve that... and given the chance, I'm going to earn yer trust."

He purses his lips but doesn't say anything more.

"I am of two minds of what should happen next," I say. "One is that we should take things slowly and maybe kiss and talk things through."

"That sounds nice. What is your other thought?"

"Whether or not you would let me undress you, so I can give you an intimate apology and suck ye off."

His eyes widen and he nods. "I would—I will—you can."

The hasty excitement behind his words makes me chuckle. "Weel, all right then. I'll make things up to ye fer a bit and then we'll talk things through after."

"Yes, please."

I can't hold back my chuckle as I lift onto my knees and tug on the bottom edge of his shirt. He sits up enough that I can pull it over his head and off his muscular arms.

Next, I undo his pants and pull them down his powerful thighs. He raises his hips and I free his feet and toss them to the floor. The fact that he doesn't have any underwear on just makes my job easier.

And how hot is that?

My clothes don't last long either—though I *am* wearing underwear—so I strip down to my boxers and keep my cock tucked away for the moment so I don't lose focus.

This is Shift's moment.

I prowl up the length of his body, my cat pacing close beneath the surface. I press my palms into the mattress on either side of his head and claim his mouth for a long, slow kiss.

Our time in the forest was rough and frenzied. I don't want that for him this time.

This time, I will show him what it means to be appreciated. And so I take my time, nipping and teasing, brushing my tongue along the seam of his lips and then playing the part of dueling swords in his mouth when he lets me in.

His hands are warm on my ribs as he holds me in place, and I'm pleased to feel that he has stopped trembling. Good. I don't want him to be afraid of what's happening between us.

"I could kiss yer lips forever," I whisper, hating to give up his mouth. "But I believe I promised ye an intimate apology."

Shift's gaze locks with mine and I wonder how the hell I've been able to resist him this long. "Do ye have any requests?"

He swallows, his cheeks flushing pink. "No. Anything involving us and this bed and being naked together is perfect."

I agree.

Straddling his hips, I sit across his thighs and run a teasing touch down the smooth planes of his chest, over the rippled moguls of his abs, and down to the sinful muscled 'V' from his hips to his cock.

And man, what a cock it is.

"I'm not sure which of yer scientists was in charge of yer man parts, but someone should give them a feckin' gold star. Hands-down yer the most perfect man I've ever seen."

His thumb brushes over the peaked point of his nipple and I can't tell if he's intensionally teasing me or if it's just him exploring his own body as I take in the show. Either way, I just about cream my boxers before we even get to the good stuff.

"Do ye like to play with yer wee nipple, lad?"

He glances down and stops.

"Och, no. Don't stop on my account. In fact, I think ye should give yerself a gentle pinch and twist. See how that feels."

He does as I tell him and his cock jumps against his abdomen. "Liked that, did ye?"

He swallows and bites his bottom lip again. "It sent a zing of pleasure through me."

"Aye, I noticed. Now, don't be shy. If ye want to play while I entertain myself by watchin', go ahead."

We spend a few more minutes with him teasing the tight buds and me getting more and more amped up. When I can't take it any longer, I shift further down the bed and take his cock into my palm.

A groan rasps from his throat when I drop my head and meet his gaze. "I am truly sorry fer bein' a stubborn arse. Please accept my apology."

My lips part over his cock and I suck his shaft deep into my mouth.

"Oh, *sweet overloading systems!*"

I chuckle. I made my super soldier utter an expletive. Well... an expletive for him.

The taste of him, sweet and slightly minty, laces my tongue. I suction around his shaft and start a slow bob from the rounded head down toward the base of his pelvis.

Shift hisses and fists the covers. "There is nothing in my enhanced programming files that accurately covers this."

No. I don't suppose there is.

I continue, pleased that my attentions have such a profound effect on him. His skin is hot and smooth in my mouth, as I glide over the solid shaft of his erection. I pause at the top of my stroke and swirl my tongue through the pearly cream weeping from his slit.

Definitely minty.

Between the flavor and the sculptured perfection and the stunning endowment... whoever designed him was more than a scientist—they were truly invested in perfection.

"Connor Mac?" He flexes forward, his hands gripping both sides of my head. I think he's trying to urge me away, but I can't tell because every time my lips slide toward his crown, he pumps back into my mouth and groans again. "I won't last, but I don't want this to end."

I chuckle and pop off for a moment to address his concerns. "There won't be an end even if ye come, lad. Trust me, this is just my apology. We haven't even gotten to the make-up sex yet."

His eyes grow wide. "There will be more?"

"Plenty more. Why do ye think I brought the food and drink in? We won't have to leave this room until tomorrow if we don't want to."

The smile that earns me is too much.

"Now, let me get back to my apology. I believe I was suckin' ye off to release."

He nods and then flops back to the pillow. "Yes, yes, you were."

With that settled, I return my focus and devour him. And yes... it's magical. There is definitely something at play here and I'm past trying to figure out what it is.

This is where we are and Shift is who I want.

When his breath hitches and his hips convulse, warm, minty cream hits my tongue.

I groan as I swallow it down... I purr as I lap up every drop of cream, like the good kitty I am.

My power surges inside me, my animal side roaring at the

taste of my mate's pleasure. I suckle and swallow, licking every drop Shift gives me.

"Ye taste good, my sweet soldier boy."

He grins. "I like that."

I chuckle and wipe my mouth with the back of my wrist. "Ye like what? Me suckin' ye off?"

"Oh, yes, I like that too, but I was referring to me being your sweet soldier boy. I like that."

The growl that vibrates from my chest is all my cat, but for once, we're in total agreement. I run my hand between his thighs and palm his balls. His cock twitches on his abdomen and stirs back to life.

"Now, do ye want to talk things through or play a little more?"

He waggles his brow and then, in a move so swift and strong I don't even know it's happening, he flips me on my back. "I want to play."

CHAPTER FIFTEEN

Mac

Our respite at Mount Nekko ends sooner than I like, but I am thankful for the break in chaos. I spent my time working with Lark on her training, with Tundra and Dune on their plans for the Amberloq trials, with Lukas strategizing about Brass and his army, and most importantly... with Shift, setting things right.

Why I'm such a stubborn arse at times boggles even me. I saw what bonding magic did for others, and yet I thought I should buck the system?

I chuckle at my audacity.

Not that it's an issue now. Shift and I spent the entire day locked away in my quarters yesterday and worked through many, if not all, of my concerns.

Sadly, real life demands our time and attention, and the quadrant of Dornte needs a defensive force. The Amberloq trials are set to start this morning and only the last details are yet to be in place.

We have shown the Elbirfae kids that live with Honor and

her mates some basic skills to practice. They are practically busting their buttons, being able to work with the weapons available.

Alpha and Beta were good sports about being interviewed by Lukas and me while Josie ran through their files for a full vetting.

Like Flash, Shift, and Link, their prime directive is to serve the Thornebanes and fight with the Amberloq to enhance the Dornte defenses. Link seems to be the only one questioning that directive. The others seem set on finding their place and serving their quadrant.

That's good. That's the right answer.

Link is the wildcard.

While I believe he wants to serve Honor and the quadrant, the past twelve years of being judged and dismissed by Andras Brass have left him skeptical and untrusting.

It'll take some doing to gain his trust and keep him on our side in the coming weeks. It might be easier if he had bonded with Lark like the other two, but from what Shift told me of the fight he had with Flash and Lark, he's holding out on that as well.

"Mac, duck!"

I turn in time to catch the blur of a projectile coming straight for my chest. My cat reflexes engage and I spring back, avoiding the arrow that narrowly misses piercing me.

With adrenaline pumping in my veins, I straighten and raise a brow toward the kids standing with their mouths hanging open. "Can someone tell me why I nearly got skewered just now?"

Skye pushes forward, and Yarko is close on her heels, as usual. "Sorry, Mac. Dune told them not to work on tackles and hand-to-hand near the archery training. The guys just got caught up and bumped into someone taking a shot. Totally not his fault, though. It was an accident."

"Won't happen again," Yarko assures me.

Dune comes jogging over and frowns at the arrow sticking into the wall of the lodge. "Who did that?"

By the look on Danner's face and the fact that he drops the bow from his hand like it's on fire, I'm guessing it was him.

I pull the tip free from the building and give the kids a warning look. "The lads were practicin' and the shot went a wee bit wide. No harm done."

"A wee bit wide?" Dune looks from the hole where the arrow pierced the wooden wall, back to where the archery targets sit, and back again. "Are you kidding me right now?"

"It was an accident," Skye says, stepping forward.

I raise my hand for her to stop. "Back to practice, kids. It seems ye have much to improve upon so, focus and do better. Aye?"

"Aye," they say, embracing the opportunity of an out and retreating in a rush. I chuckle at them mimicking my accent, but take no offense.

They're good kids and they've been through a lot to survive that damnable goblin prison camp. If they are overly excited to become warriors and reclaim a bit of their self-confidence, I can't blame them a bit.

Dune still doesn't look pleased.

Which is actually hilarious because, from what I know about the man, he's been a giant kid screw up the past many years. Maybe being mated to Honor and given a leadership role transformed him into a pinnacle of focus and maturity.

Or maybe he's trying hard to be a better man and a better soldier for his mates.

I can't fault the guy for that.

Tundra and Lark land beside us, and Lark's expression darkens. "What is it? What's wrong?"

"Och, it's nothin', lass. Just kids gettin' the feel of things in a world very different from what they're accustomed to. It'll take time to settle in and figure out what warriors they'll be."

She studies my expression and seems satisfied. "Training isn't entirely new to them. For the two years we were captives, they were taught strategy and defense, as well as fighting skills."

I nod. "I have no doubt they did the best in the time and space they had to work with, but bein' here is different. They've got open space and access to weapons without the fear of being discovered and punished. It's an exciting time for them."

Tundra is watching the kids, worry clouding his gaze. "The other applicants will begin arriving shortly. Not all of them will make it to the end."

"No, but that doesn't mean they're out of the runnin' entirely. Ye lowered the age of eligibility fer these trials, did ye not?"

"We did. We also opened it up to all fae races and sects."

Dune nods. "The Amberloq is not just for the Elbirfae any longer."

I think that's the best decision. By keeping the parameters so restrictive, they likely turned away a lot of soldiers committed to help protect the Crown.

With their entire force being dwindled to the three of them and, by extension of marriage, Lukas and our teams, they need as many soldiers as they can pull together.

The rhythmic beat of rotor blades cutting through the morning sky draws our attention to the silver reflection in the distance. Lukas made the rounds at the crack of dawn, picking up applicants from the farther reaches of the quadrant. Now we'll send Yarko back to Thornebane Castle to portal any others who showed up eager to join.

"And it begins," I say.

Lark nods, glancing over to where the three are sparring with Alpha and Beta. "I hope they do all right."

"They don't have to prove themselves as warriors," Tundra

says. "With them, we're focusing more on their ability to work with others and follow orders."

I've worked hard on not getting drawn in by my attraction to Shift over the past couple of days, but after yesterday, watching him move—his bare skin glistening in the sun as he trains—is too much for my willpower to fight.

A long sigh of contentment escapes my lungs before I can get control of myself.

Tundra and Dune have broken off to have a side conversation and don't seem to notice. Lark does and sends me a knowing smile. "They are just too damned good to look at, aren't they?"

I drop my gaze and toe the dirt with my boot. "How are things... ye know, with them? Shift mentioned Link causin' a rift. He said he spouted off pretty good and did some damage."

She lifts a shoulder. "I'm thinking that's just Link. He hasn't wrapped his head around letting people into his circle, so he's making sure no one slips in there unexpectedly."

"But yer all right?"

She bumps my shoulder with her wing and chuckles. "It will take more than a few insults and a dose of male arrogance to hurt me. I'm fine. I was angry more than hurt. I just want the best for them and Link doesn't see it."

"Aye, but he will. I've had tough nuts on my team before and given enough time and space, they always seem to come around."

She casts me a teasing smirk. "Speaking of coming around, I see you and Shift have turned a corner."

I can't help but smile when I take him in across the training yard. Then I remember I'm a professional in a field of fighters and lock my shit down.

Lark laughs. "You don't have to pretend with me. If there is one person who understands how strange it is to be falling for an automaton, it's me."

Aye, I suppose that's true. "Has he said anythin' about us? About our... yesterday?"

She shakes her head. "No, but the sadness and worry in his eyes has cleared, and he didn't come to our suite last night, so I hoped."

My first instinct is to keep my business private, but what's the sense? As bizarre as it is, we're all in this tangled mess of emotions together. "Aye, weel, it took a bit, but I got my head out of my arse and set things right with him. We're still navi-gatin' what it all means, but I'm off the fence and I'm done pretendin' he's not the one I want."

She bursts into a glorious smile. "I'm so happy for the two of you. Welcome to the weirdness of loving bio-engineered men."

Love? I wouldn't go that far, but I understand her point. We're together in an undeniable bond. It's more than dating, but less than a lifelong promise.

It's building something that feels right.

My cat growls, prowling within me. If it were up to my animal side, we'd accept the bond and claim him as our mate right now.

It's too soon.

I have my life back in the Human Realm to sort out, a squad I'm proud to lead to consider, and a vision of my future I need to reassess.

It occurs to me too late that I've let the conversation drop and when I glance over at Lark, there's worry in those green eyes of hers.

Before I can play off her concern, she wraps her arms around my ribs and pulls me into a tight hug. I'm taken off guard for a moment, but then I realize it's been way too long since I held a woman in my arms. The past year has been all about Hawk's father coming after the realm, then the attacks on Keyla and her mates, and then Lukas needing to take down the forces coming after Honor.

I thrive on being needed in a dangerous situation, but yeah, it's taken its toll. I accept the comfort as it's meant and then ease back.

She holds up a finger. "Before you give me the whole, 'warriors don't hug warriors' speech, let me just say that as your friend, you needed that."

I swallow and rake a hand through my hair. "Aye, maybe I did."

"Do me a favor and take a deep breath."

I arch a brow and give her a sidelong look. "Why?"

"Trust me for a moment. Close your eyes and take a deep breath."

I'm not sure what she's getting at, but I do. With my eyes closed, I draw a deep breath, filling my lungs to their depths.

"Again. This time, take note of what you smell."

All right. I exhale, shake out my muscles a bit, and draw another long breath in.

The first thing I smell is Lark. Her scent, like all the Elbirfae, carries a hint of her home biome. She smells like cedar and affection... and sex with Flash.

My cat growls, but I push him back down. *That's none of our business.* Lark gave me the opportunity to weigh in on having a sexual relationship with them and I lost my temper.

"What do you smell?"

I shake myself inwardly and focus on her question. "I smell you, the mountain air, and the excitement of the young ones."

"And what do you hear?"

"The helicopter is close and the combat training has stopped, likely so the kids can watch the strange silver bird land."

"All right. Now, what do you feel?"

I blink open one of my eyes and she waggles a finger at me. "No cheating. Close your eyes and tell me what you feel."

I do as I'm told, take another deep breath, and relax into the moment. "I feel the vibration of the air displaced by the rotor blades. I feel the warmth of yer body close to mine. And I feel the nervous anxiety of what is coming."

Warm hands encircle my wrists and I open my eyes to face Lark standing directly in front of me. "That nervous anxiety is hope. It's the hope of kids who lived through trauma and want to be more than what happened to them. It's the hope Dune, Tundra, and I share that we can resurrect a dominant force of warriors to protect Dornte. And it's the hope of five discarded men who want to find a home and build a life with the people who have done nothing but treat them like they are nothing."

Our gazes lock. "What is yer point, lass?"

"Right here and right now, we're at the precipice of something completely new. It has the potential to be great, but there's no telling how it will turn out. Will these be the warriors we need? Will the people who come here succeed or fail? Will we carve a new future out based on the relationships built over the next week? I don't know, but I'm open to see what that future might look like."

My gaze flicks over the rise of her wing to where Shift has stopped training across the lawn. Instead of working out with his brothers, he's now watching the two of us.

Lark squeezes my wrists and smiles. "You're a brave and heroic man, Mac. You risk your life for those who can't defend themselves and you'll die for your friends and what you believe in. You can be brave with him, too."

I arch a brow at her, but her words strike home, and she knows it.

"I know you're still worrying about the details, but meet the potential. The universe wants you in this with us. I'm thrilled the two of you are moving toward something, but try not to worry about the fine points. They'll work themselves out."

I grunt. "Simple as that, is it?"

She dips her chin. "Your reasons for worrying are valid—no argument. You're doing most, if not all the sacrificing—and that's hard. But think of all the reasons this is worth the risk: devoted partners, a strong and skilled combat force to share dangers in battle, found family, a new realm and a quadrant that needs people to really make a difference, and at the risk of over-sharing—the sex."

Her eyes roll back and she gives off a waft of sexual energy. Thankfully, I think I'm the only shifter in the group, so no one else needs to be privy to her arousal. "Let's just say that their heightened abilities are fully activated and their data programming is incredibly thorough."

My cat prowls closer and I draw another long breath into my lungs. Fuck, her arousal is intoxicating.

Her Cheshire smile is way too sexy.

"Are ye maybe referin' to Shift's molecular manipulation and how that plays out in sexual applications?"

Her smile blows my mind.

I chuckle and realize my boxers are getting tighter and this is neither the time nor the place to be growing a cockstand. "Och, now yer just causin' trouble."

When I tug at my pants and adjust my stance, she laughs. "Okay, enough said. I'm just thrilled to have you in the mix."

The helicopter moves directly overhead, and I wrap an arm around the back of her hips and escort her out of the way. I'm not sure how I feel about being in the mix. Then again, it's too late now.

CHAPTER SIXTEEN

Lark

𝒶fter the helicopter unloads and Yarko returns with the warrior hopefuls who showed up at Amberloq Hall, Dune, Tundra, and I greet the thirty-eight applicants and assemble them in the grand entrance of the Amberloq lodge. There's a great deal of excitement and I'm looking forward to seeing what everyone can do. Since I've never been through the training, they are going to handle the lion's share of the events.

I will oversee the five super soldiers and ensure their transition into the Amberloq ranks goes smoothly. And while I told Mac that the Elbirfae kids are excited to get past what happened to them and to see who they can become, so too are the five.

Alpha and Beta have fewer social nuances than Flash, Shift, and Link, but they are no less capable as fighters. They are eager to please, and even more eager to be considered a value to the Amberloq force.

Link, Shift, and Flash are also motivated to prove themselves, but they want more than what they were created for. It's obvious they were given a greater range of adaptability, especially when considering the building of relationships: the bonding between brothers-in-arms, the cultivation of friendships and romantic entanglements, and the respect of accepting direction and orders from their superiors.

In fact, despite our fight, even Link seems to be doing better in that department. He engaged with Skye and Yarko the other night and Dune said the two of them sat and talked over drinks.

I can't help but hope that's a good sign.

Tundra raises a hand to quiet the chatter and addresses the group. "Welcome, everyone. To begin, let's get you settled. All of you who just arrived can claim a room on the second floor for the week. The young Elbirfae are on three and you likely will get more rest on your own floor. Place your belongings in one of the rooms with an open door, and then change into workout clothes and meet us on the training grounds in twenty minutes."

The new arrivals hustle up the stairs while the rest of us watch them go.

Moving into the group of Elbirfae kids, I lay my arm over River's shoulder and scan their expressions. "Why do you look so worried?"

Danner meets my gaze. "Did you see the size of some of those men? They look like military machines."

Skye laughs. "What's the matter, guys? Are you scared of the competition?"

By the look on their faces, I'd have to say they are.

"Okay, listen up." I clap my hands together gently to tear their attention from the stairs. "The twenty of you have been practicing for years and have been here all day. You've got the lay of the land. You've been training with not only us, but also the five. Being here and taking part in the trials isn't a competition pitting you against those new arrivals."

"Thank the gods for that," Lief says.

The group lets off a stressful chuckle.

I sweep a hand through the air, gesturing to them. "Being

here is about rising to the call of what we need you to be to protect our quadrant. Pay attention during the drills. Show Tundra and Dune what you're made of. Focus on why you're here and what you want from this opportunity. Got it?"

They all give me a nod.

"Be great and earn your place as Amberloq warriors. It's as simple as that."

They nod again.

"Now, go out there and shine. There's not one of you that doesn't deserve to be an Amberloq. And listen, if it isn't this time around, you're young and you have many more years to make it happen."

Stone and Storm, twins from the desert biome, let out a cheer and they pump their fists into the air as they march off.

Skye giggles, watching them go and moves to stand next to me. She's not only too young to be considered, but being Tundra's ward, she'd probably give him an aneurysm if she decided to be a warrior. "They're going to be great. You'll see."

I wrap an arm around her wings and pull her to my side. "I have no doubt. Come on. Let's go watch the warm up event."

Flash

As THE NEW applicants filter down from putting their belongings away to gather on the training lawn, my brothers and I stand back and assess the competition. Yes, no matter what Lark believes, being created as the elite soldiers means that anyone else vying for the same position as us *is* competition.

Will they challenge us?

Will they try to discredit us?

Will they wish to prove themselves better fighters than the so-called 'super soldiers'?

The twenty kids from the goblin prison camp won't be an issue. They are young, eager to learn, they idolize Lark, and they respect her as their leader. They also think we're 'cool'.

Once Lark informed us that cool was a term of appreciation and admiration, we were pleased.

So, out of the gathered thirty-eight applicants, twenty of them are the Elbirfae kids, five are us, and then there are thirteen unknown quantities to assess and ultimately outperform.

We accept the challenge.

Link opens our private channel of our neuro-communication and, giving nothing away, passes a gaze over the field of competition. *There are five of us and thirteen opponents to assess over the course of the next few days. Record interactions and observations and we'll compile our files and discuss each evening.*

Shift dips his chin and despite his attention being locked on a conversation between Lark and Mac, he acknowledges Link's orders.

I nod. *I will inform Alpha and Beta of our plans. Do you believe you will one day be able to include them in our neuro-link?*

I don't know. If Lukas will allow me access to the bunker's server, I might. If not, I don't think it will be possible.

That would be a shame, both personally and while battling as brothers-in-arms.

Agreed.

Dune presses his fingers into his mouth and lets off a long whistle, raising his other hand. "Everyone, fall in."

The five of us join the assembled fighters.

Tundra, Dune, and Lark make an impressive sight, standing tall at the front of the group.

Tundra, by far, is the most imposing of the three, with his height, his muscular frame, and his pale skin and ebony hair standing in stark contrast. As he presents himself, the group takes in his snow-white wings flecked with black. They rise over the rounds of his broad shoulders and even relax against his back. It's clear they are powerful weapons.

Dune stands taller and more serious than I've ever seen him. Usually the joker of the group, he seems to have set aside his playful antics today. Even with his hair long and falling in a mess of gold around his rich, brown horns, no one would guess he's anything other than a stern and serious warrior. He smiles at the group, giving everyone a moment to take in his toned physique and his sand and brown falcon feathers.

And then there is my lovely, Lark. Standing tall with her ebony wings draping down behind the curves of her breasts, waist, and hips, she is all feminine power. Her eyes are as bright as the greenest gemstone and when she takes in the group, I am incredibly proud to know this female is mine.

When everyone has sized one another up, Dune begins his address. "Welcome. I am Dune, this is Tundra, and that is Lark. We are the Dornte Biome Generals and your superiors. We are the ones who will observe and assess your suitability to become Amberloq warriors. I doubt all of you will make it through, but we thank you for taking the time to come all this way and try. Good luck."

The group ebbs a little under the sobering thought that they might not make it through, but no one seems overly discouraged.

Tundra speaks next. "We know you're excited to show your strengths and prove you were born to be a warrior with the Amberloq, but let me make one thing clear: we do not owe you a spot on our force. Yes, our numbers are depleted and yes, we are eager to fill our barracks once again to ensure we can protect our quadrant, but we will take no one who won't be a good fit with our unit."

He glances over to Lark, who smiles and takes her turn, addressing the group. "This is a time of firsts. I am the first female Biome General in history. It's the first time the age of application has been lowered, and it's the first time members of other races and sects have been invited to join our ranks. That being said, a non-cohesive warrior, no matter his or her fighting skills, is more likely to get one of us killed than help in a battle. So, when Tundra speaks of you needing to be a good fit, understand that we're looking for more than fighters."

My chest warms with pride and I feel the same surge of warmth across the bond shared with my brothers. I'm not surprised Shift feels that way. He has embraced our catalyst connection as fully as I have.

What surprises me is that I feel the same rush of pride and approval from Link.

Though Link's expression shows no outward attachment to Lark, he was the first to taste her blood, the first to feel the effects of the catalyst unlocking his powers, and the one most resistant to the idea of our forming a relationship with her.

The warmth I'm feeling from him is not only heartening, it's a good sign.

Perhaps our fight got through to him.

Link is guarded but once you earn a place at his side, you are his evermore.

Dune gestures toward the flat grounds bordered by the high stone fence. "These are our training grounds. All our physical training and trials will be held out here. For now, Tundra will lead you in the exercises and formations. Learn them. Practice them. And commit them to your daily routine because attacks come at any time and you need to have your body and mind ready for engagement. Understood?"

We all nod.

"Good. Then watch and learn. We look forward to seeing how you do."

∾

Lark

THE FIRST DAY of the trials starts with physical evaluations of fitness, psychological games of strategy, and learning the training exercises and fighting stance formations. Tundra and Dune exhibit endless patience, setting the applicants into proper positions and ensuring they understand the importance of the motions of the formations.

It's fun to see this side of them.

In the afternoon, we move on to basic one-on-one holds and sparring. They aren't free to spar, but are walked through the offensive and defensive strategies for close-quarter assaults.

The five likely know all this, but remain engaged.

My kids from the goblin camp absorb every word and nuance with full focus, and I couldn't be prouder.

And bit by bit, I learn the names and faces of the warriors I only met this morning.

The second day of the trials focuses on de-escalation strategies, disarming opponents, and the importance of protecting citizens from collateral violence. Tundra and Dune spend hours in the classroom with them going over psychological cues and triggers to help them read situations. Then they demonstrate and work with the applicants on a one-on-one basis.

And like yesterday, I oversee and observe.

To the applicants, I'm evaluating. To everyone who knows better, my fighting skills aren't finely tuned enough to measure up to what would be considered 'Amberloq standards'.

Still, I've earned my place and will prove to them I belong here. I may not be at the top of my game yet, but during our downtime, I've been working with Tundra, Dune, Mac, and the soldiers to get stronger.

By the third day, the applicants are excited to finally show their combat skills.

"Good morning," I say when everyone finishes their formation exercises and stretching. "Today we're shifting focus to weapons and hand-to-hand combat. Dune will oversee weapons, and Tundra is on melee fighting."

There's a rush of excitement from the Elbirfae kids and I shoot them a look to remind them they are still being evaluated.

I hold my hand straight out, using my flexed fingers to show me slicing through the center of the group. "This group head over to the left, the rest of you to the right. Count it out so there are nineteen per side and you can pair off evenly."

Everyone seems to understand my instructions and breaks off accordingly.

I follow the half that goes over to Tundra first, holding the data pad we've been using for assessments.

"Today we'll be testing your close quarter fighting skills," Tundra says. "You'll be evaluated based on the proficiency of your movement, the outcome of the pairing, and your innovation and decorum in combat. Remember, this is a sparring drill. Yes, we want to see what you can do, but we're all friends here. When I pair you off for your match, remember who I pit you against."

While Tundra moves forward, indicating who will fight whom, Mac and Lukas come to stand beside me. The two of them have been working out of the war room for the past two days, researching the information they gained during the interrogation of the Gen-3 soldiers.

We haven't seen much of them.

I hope that means they're getting somewhere and are tracking down Andras Brass and the rogue Gen-3 super soldiers.

"How are things?" Lukas asks, casting a surveying glance over at the group. "Is anyone standing out?"

I tap on my screen and pull up the leaderboard. "The top ten are in no particular order."

He scans the list of names for a minute and then lifts his gaze. "I'm not surprised to find our five bunker soldiers ranking highly. Oh, and Yarko's doing well too."

I nod. "His portaling ability gave him a strong advantage during the de-escalation and citizen protection exercises. During the roleplay of several standoffs, he flashed in behind the hostile force and simply removed the innocents from the equation."

Mac chuckles. "That's one way to do it."

Lukas grins. "Where was he all those times we were pinned down and getting our asses kicked?"

"Aye, that's a good question."

Tundra has the groups divided and asks them to space out with their partner.

"Point out the others for us, so we can keep watch too," Lukas says.

Glancing down at the names, I search the training field and find the ones to watch.

"Two of them are in combat and two are in weapons. In this group, Kezay is the satyr and Alryx-Ti is the mountain elf."

They locate the two and settle in beside me to watch what happens next.

Tundra finishes addressing them. "All right. You will face off against your designated partner one group at a time. Full contact is expected. I will cue you to start and you will fight until one of you either concedes or is unconscious. If I believe one of you might be harmed beyond the scope of this exercise, I will command you to 'hold'. If I call hold, you will stop immediately. Am I clear?"

They all nod.

Tundra steps back and signals for the first pairing to come forward. As the other applicants step back to give them space to fight, Beta and Alryx-Ti step into the circle.

"The mountain elves in this realm are much bigger than

those found in the Human Realm," Lukas says, taking in the burly fighter. He hasn't got the muscled bulk of Beta but he certainly doubles the size of a grove or meadow elf.

Beta stops in the center of the circle facing Alryx-Ti and gives him a ceremonial bow. Alryx-Ti returns the gesture and then stands tall and confident in his stance.

"When you're ready," Tundra says.

Beta is nearly statue still as Alryx-Ti raises his hands in a defensive posture. He stretches his neck, bouncing on the balls of his feet, ready for Beta to strike at a moment's notice.

"It's interesting that in a test of warrior strengths, he chose a defensive stance," Lukas says.

It's not common knowledge that Beta and Alpha are engineered soldiers, but it's not a secret either.

Mac nods. "Aye. I was thinkin' the same thing. Either he knows what Beta is and doesn't want to over commit or he's got enough patience and self-assurance to let things play out."

I hadn't thought of it that way. My first instinct was that he might feel intimidated by Beta, but maybe they're right. Maybe he's confident enough to see what Beta can do.

I chastise myself for jumping to the obvious conclusion and make a mental note to ask Mac to help me with my strategic assessment. All my experience with battle has either been fight or flight to survive. That's where my first instincts go, but I want to have a more well-rounded understanding of why an opponent might do the things they do.

The stand-off assessment only lasts so long before Alryx-Ti engages. He cuts the distance between them, moving swiftly and without hesitation. His arms flick out with the graceful efficiency of his elven blood, followed by well-honed sweeps and kicks from his long legs.

Beta absorbs the attack, allowing Alryx-Ti's aggression to take them back and forth across the field. The two are both calm, intellectual fighters and I realize that for every dodge

Alryx-Ti lands, and every blow Beta parries, the two are evaluating one another.

"They fight differently than goblins," I say.

Mac nods. "Och, lass. Goblins are not fighters. They are malicious thugs who use leverage and brutality to get their way. There is no honor or skill in that. No, when you come against a true warrior, even if yer guts twist and burn with hatred, there is always a sliver of respect fer the skills they possess."

Lukas' head bobs absently as they watch.

The challenges between the two are becoming harsher and the smack of fist to flesh and the grunts of men being knocked off their stride grow in the air.

"They're both good," Lukas says.

"Aye, they are."

"Beta is holding back."

"I suppose that's a good thing. We still don't know the full extent of what those boys can do."

"But we should." Lukas sighs, casting a glance from where Flash and Shift are watching Beta's match and then over to where Alpha and Link are interacting with Dune's weapon group. "Midnight tonight, round the five of them up and we'll meet in the gym. I think we need a full demonstration of their abilities."

I nod. "Okay. I'll let them know."

CHAPTER SEVENTEEN

Mac

The three of us continue to assess the fighters and I admit, they've got a talented group. Not everyone is battle ready, but there is definite potential. The kids need the most work, but of the thirteen random applicants who showed up, there are some solid skills in the mix.

"Shift and Kezay," Tundra calls, bringing forth the next pairing.

I take stock of the satyr Shift will face and the hair on the back of my neck raises.

Kezay is one of the more experienced fighters. Though his fae race makes it difficult to tell his age, by the way he holds his stance and takes in his opponent, it's easy to see he's accustomed to battle.

"Are the satyrs of this realm normally fighters?" I ask. "In our realm, they're passive."

Lark sighs, frowning at the male before us. "The satyrs have been at war among themselves for generations. They fight over land, females, property, pride... pretty much any excuse for bloodshed."

"Aye, we have a few sects like that in the Human Realm, too."

I eye up the male. My cat dislikes him on principle—he wants to hurt Shift. It's there in his mossy green eyes and the way he paws his hoof at the ground like he's an angry bull about to charge.

Tall and wiry, he's bare to the navel with a thick pelt of silver and brown fur from his hips down to his hooves. With sticks and leaves poking out of the wild shock of green hair that cascades around a short rack of antlers and then his face, he looks like he's been caught in a windstorm and tumbled across a forest floor, gathering debris.

Despite this, he wears an air of power, something that only comes from recurring success on the battlefield. I don't like it.

"Easy." Lukas grips my wrist and tugs me backward by my arm. "Down, tiger."

Shit. I cut off the growl and root my boots to the spot. I didn't realize I was moving. Shaking out my limbs, I step back in line with him and Lark. "Sorry about that."

Lark sends me a sympathetic smile. "You don't have to apologize. By the way, I think you just made Shift's day."

I meet Shift's warm caramel gaze and feel my cheeks flame hot. He's way too aware of my reaction. Stupid Celtic complexion. I can't hide a damn thing when embarrassed.

And I *am* embarrassed.

I know better than to doubt what the three can do. Lark and I have battled with and against them, and they are tactically flawless and physically brutal warriors. "My reaction makes no sense."

"Your reaction makes perfect sense," Lukas says, casting me a sidelong grin. "You're in luuurve."

"Fuck off."

Lukas chuckles. "Fine. I'll keep my opinions to myself. I'm

just saying that you've been a helluva lot more pleasant the past three days than you were the three before that. If that temple of male perfection keeps you from tossing off alone in the shower, I say embrace what's happening and dig in."

"Is that you keeping yer opinions to yerself?"

He laughs and fixes his eyes straight ahead.

Yeah, I fucking well thought so.

The match between Shift and Kezay has begun and the two of them circle one another, assessing the strengths opposing them and the openings to take advantage of. With Shift, I don't see any openings.

The guy is one solid fighter.

And a beautiful thing to watch.

I know he can take care of himself, and yet the twisting in my gut makes me want to step into the line of fire and shield him from what's coming.

The emotion is unsettling.

I've been going into conflicts with my squads for over a decade now, and I never feel like this. It's worrisome and could be dangerous and distracting in battle. It's definitely something I'll need to address and come to terms with.

Then again, both Lukas and Hawk seem able to fight with their mates at their sides.

Hawk was homicidal and obsessive at first with Calli, but they seemed to get through it. And Lukas doesn't seem to have a problem with Honor fighting.

Maybe I just need time to get used to the idea.

Shift can certainly take care of himself.

Is it because of the bond I share with Shift? Would I feel any different if Lark was in that fighting circle? Or Flash? Or Link?

Even without looking, I feel Lark's presence humming like a soothing vibration in my bones. Aside from her being tall, dark, and gorgeous, she's got the heart of a warrior and a kindness that survived her ordeal and only made her warmer and more accepting.

Drawing in a deep breath, I let her feminine scent permeate my senses. She has an earthy, cedar scent that I'm growing quite fond of. And her carrying Shift's scent on her skin makes my cock twitch... in a good way.

I scan the training grounds and study Link and Flash next. I could take or leave Link, but Flash might be a different story. He's at least open and honest about what's going on with him.

Man, there are so many parts and pieces to this.

Leaning to the side, I lower my voice so only Lukas hears me. "Doesn't havin' five in a relationship get overwhelmin'? It seems like it would be a lot to keep track of."

Thankfully, Lukas doesn't make fun. He lifts one shoulder and scrubs a hand over his mouth, covering his words. "It was a bit of an emotional clusterfuck in the beginning, but once it clicked, it really clicked."

I've never made it work with one partner. How do I make it work when the guy I'm drawn to is part of a foursome already?

My mind is tumbling with those questions as I continue to watch Shift fight. Fuck, he's a beautifully made male... all that corded strength and honed muscle pulling and flexing with each block and strike.

And yeah, now I'm getting hard.

Dammit. The last thing I need is to be throwing wood on the training grounds with forty people here to see me swooning over one of the applicants.

Maybe I should go watch Dune's group work on weapon proficiency. At least until the pressure behind my fly dies down.

I'm about to excuse myself when I notice the faint smirk curling up one corner of Kezay's mouth. There's a flash of something dark in his eyes and everything in me knows he's about to attack.

And not in the sense of the sparring match.

My instincts fire hot in my blood and I step forward to intervene. The moment the satyr opens his mouth, Shift's eyes roll into the back of his head.

I'm running before his knees have even hit the ground, my heavy footfalls pounding out a punishing rhythm.

"Hold," Tundra shouts, pushing forward.

But the fucker isn't holding and from the look in his eye, he has no intention of releasing Shift from whatever he's doing.

Flash drops to the ground next.

And then Beta.

Fuck. Whatever sonic dog whistle attack he's got going on, it's shutting down the supers.

"Move!" I snarl, not slowing down as I get to the ring of applicants. My adrenaline is firing in my veins, my entire body vibrating with my need to protect.

As I break into the circle and see Shift helpless on the ground, my cat paces wildly within me, my skin crawling with the olfactory offense of his pain.

The roar that tears from my throat is nothing short of murderous and in the moment I hang in the air, claws extended, I have the satisfaction of seeing the fucker's smug smirk fall.

That's right, asshole. I'm here for you.

My claws have fully extended beyond my nail beds and my fangs have dropped. I take the satyr down in a tangle of flailing limbs and flashing fangs. He will pay for trying to take what is mine.

That's right—*mine.*

Shift

My systems come back online, my sensory inputs bombarding me with scrambled sights, snarling sounds, and a surreal sense of urgency. Blood is spraying through the air and it takes a moment for my mental processing to catch up with what I'm seeing.

Mac straightens, his chest heaving with labored breaths, the bloody body of Kezay discarded on the turf at his feet.

"Mac? What is it? What happened?"

When he looks at me, he stands on two legs, but the man is tormented and his features are distorted. His Sith cat is present in the glow of his eyes, the curves of his claws, the points of his fangs, and the eerie growl filling the air around us. Standing over me, with his red curls hanging wild around his face, I am struck with a need for him that blinds me to all else.

I struggle to get to my knees.

The world tilts and, as much as I want to go to him, my motor functions aren't engaging.

I see the panicked gazes passing between the Elbirfae kids and then find Lark curled over Flash.

"What happened? Is Kezay dead?"

Mac lets off another long growl.

"Everyone stand your ground," Lukas snaps. "Predatory cats attack from behind and if you run, you'll only trigger him to chase. He's protecting Shift. As long as you don't go near him, you'll be fine."

Protecting me?

I meet the wildness in Mac's gaze. "Are ye all right?" His words are fractured between the man and his animal self, but his concern is obvious and warms me like a balm.

I glance toward the heap of satyr bleeding out on the grass, a raw hole left where his throat should be. "Whatever happened, it's over and I am well."

"He lost control of his Sith side when you went down," Lukas says beside me, his voice intentionally quiet and calm. "Kezay seemed to have a side agenda to take you and your brothers down. He used some kind of sonic signal to disrupt your programming."

Dune and Tundra bring Alpha and Link over to our circle. They land in the center of the group and help to keep my brothers on their feet.

"You did well, Mac," Lukas says. "Whatever Kezay was doing, it's over. You stopped him. You can stand down now."

"He cannot," I say, holding my hand up to my male. "I feel the chaos within him. His Sith side is seething."

"Okay, here's what we're going to do," Lukas says. "Shift, you need to get up and get to him. Yarko, the moment Shift has Mac in his hold, flash in behind them and portal them to Mac's quarters. I've seen this before with dominant shifters. It's nothing some private time won't cure."

Mac snarls, bearing his fangs at Lukas.

Dune chuckles. "I'm not sure Mac's kitty likes you discussing his business, magic man."

"He's just hissy. Shift, it's your move."

I take my cue and try again to get vertical. This time my body responds the way I want and I get to my feet. With my arms open and our gazes locked, I take a tentative step toward my male. "You did a tremendous job protecting my brothers and me. Thank you, Mac."

A buzz hums through me, echoing along the bond that pulls me toward him.

"*I* protected you."

I take another step closer, my balance returning and my mobility functions all coming fully online. "And you were very thorough."

Lark helps Flash to his feet, and like me, he seems to recover well. I'm relieved. Now to attend to Mac's needs. "Now, let's go somewhere private and get you cleaned up."

The moment we're within touching distance, I pull him against my chest and wrap him in a tight embrace. The rush of portal energy is strange when it hits and even stranger when my surroundings change in the snap of one second to the next.

Gone are the wide-eyed gazes of forty people.

Now there is just Mac and me, alone in his bedroom. Easing back, I ensure Yarko is gone and we are indeed alone.

We are.

Mac's tormented gaze pierces my heart.

"I don't know how to make this better for you," I say. "Tell me what you need."

He lifts me off my feet and pins me against the wall. A rough hand on my forehead presses my cheek against the drywall, and then he's licking up the column of my neck. "Mine."

My heart rate shudders, and then a hot piercing pain brings his incisors into my neck. The shock and burn of the penetration only lasts a moment and then his hand palms the front of my pants. My body's response to him is immediate, my erection thickening to meet his grip.

"Mine..." he hisses against the flesh of my neck, his tongue laving my flesh as he suckles and draws.

The carnal demand of his animal taking from me is sinfully delicious. There's no hesitation on my part.

Everything within me submits to his claim.

A quick swipe of his claw rips open the front of my pants and I thrust my hips to fill the palm of his hand. His fingers tighten around my erection.

My groan is ragged and raw as I press against him. "Yes... I am yours."

CHAPTER EIGHTEEN

Link

Kneeling over the bloody corpse of the satyr male, I'm inundated with questions. How could a satyr take down the five of us? What kind of attack shut down our processors? Why did this male want to disable us? What does it mean that Mac's Sith cat could do what we could not?

Lukas chuckles beside me. "It means despite what you think, you need to get it through your neuro-processors that you're not all that."

I didn't realize I was speaking aloud. Curious. It seems my systems aren't back to full function yet.

I frown at the human. "In no capacity of strength or skill are you my better and yet you consider yourself my superior. I find that puzzling."

He shakes his head. "In no capacity of experience or real-world conflict are you *my* better. You're a junior officer. Stop believing you're at the top of the hierarchy and you might learn something."

I consider his words but find them flawed. "The probability of that is minuscule."

He arches an eyebrow. "Did Andras Brass program you to be such an arrogant dickwad, or did you adapt into one?"

I'm unfamiliar with the term 'dickwad', but there is a ninety-nine point three percent chance it is a term of insult. "Why would a statement of fact be considered arrogance? It is true. I am a superior soldier."

He barks a laugh. "Trust me, in some aspects of soldiering, you have definite advantages. I'd never try to tell you otherwise. In other aspects, you are so ill-prepared to be part of a warrior squad, it's pathetic."

I stiffen. "Surely, you can't believe that."

He laughs again. "Oh yeah, I can, because it's abso-fucking-lutely true."

He looks over at his mates, and both Tundra and Dune are giving me the same look. "What is it the three of you believe you know which I don't?"

Lukas stretches his neck from side to side and then exhales. "Being part of a warrior squad in the real world means the soldiers you serve with have different strengths. Someone might have experience with an enemy you haven't encountered, so you'll listen and consider their input. Another soldier might've grown up in the climate or landscape you're about to infiltrate, so you accept their suggestions on approach or exfil. Their input is valuable and so you respect their place on your team."

"Even if I am the superior soldier?"

"You need to redefine your definition of what it means to be a soldier."

"I don't think I do."

Dune laughs. "Oh, you definitely do. And I can say that because it wasn't so long ago when I was standing where you are now. Once I got my head out of my ass and stepped out of my own way, that's when my world really came together."

The anatomical improbability of him having his head up his own ass or being able to step out of his own way is astounding.

Why do these people speak such nonsense?

Lukas gestures to the body of the dead applicant. "You got lucky today. Mac's Sith disabled Kezay's sonar attack before you five shut down for good. In this instance, he was the better soldier to handle what came at you. You might be stronger and designed with more gadgets, but that doesn't make you better in all instances."

"We'll work on it," Lark says, moving to my side. "For now, let's focus on Kezay and why he wanted to take you five down."

"That's a simple answer," Flash says, holding the arm of the dead applicant. "His programming demanded it. This is one of the Gen-3 models."

"What? Here?" Lark scowls, searching the training field which has been cleared of all applicants. "Why didn't we pick up on that?"

"We didn't get visual information on all twenty-six of them," Lukas says.

"Does that mean there could be more of them here?" Dune asks.

Lukas nods. "I'd bet on it. Okay, let's keep this between us for now. Any other Gen-3 soldiers here will know we're on to them, but there's no need to freak out the kids. In fact, I'll have Yarko return the kids back to Amberloq Hall, so they're out of the equation."

Lark nods. "I think we'd all feel better knowing they're safe."

Dune whistles. "They will be pissed. They've been hyped about these trials. To be kicked out when things are getting interesting will sting."

Tundra dismisses his mate's concern. "No. We'll explain our

reasoning and they will accept that. Lukas is right. The young ones need to be removed from harm's way."

"Then how do we proceed?" Lark asks, searching the faces of the others. "How will we weed out which of the remaining applicants are moles here to take down our five?"

Hearing Lark claim us is both a surprise and slightly unnerving. After the way I behaved and the things I said, I assumed I was no longer considered one of her charges.

I insulted her efforts and her relationship with my brothers. With the emotional energy that leaks through our cognitive bond when they have sex, I was very aware of her liaisons with them, but failed to assign the proper level of importance that demanded.

Sex doesn't mean loyalty.

Sex doesn't mean commitment.

And yet, despite my behavior, she speaks as protectively of us and our well-being as she ever has.

"The easiest way would be by evaluating their performance," Dune says, "but they could easily hold back so they don't stand out."

Agreed.

"Any or all of the remaining twelve could be part of Brass's Gen-3 army," Lukas says.

"Which is fine unless there's more than one that can create that sonic frequency attack," Lark says.

Lukas looks at me. "If I arrange for access to the main server where Brass and his team stored your system data, do you think you can correct whatever happened so it doesn't happen again?"

"You think he programmed them with a kill switch?" Dune asks.

"I do."

I consider the likelihood of his query and nod. "I believe Dr. Brass may have encoded our program to shut down when hit with a certain vibrational frequency. If I'm correct, then yes, I should be able to counter his intentions."

Lukas nods. "My next question is, can I trust you? You have already accessed the server frequently, and taken it upon yourself to either search, alter, or change things without authorization."

The look of mistrust is echoed around the group in the gazes of Dune and Tundra, Lark, and even Flash. I don't enjoy the sensation of their censure. "I give you my word. I will work to eliminate any back door programing Andras Brass set in place to cripple me and my brothers, and nothing more."

Flash arches a brow. "We had also discussed the possibility of extending our neuro-link to Alpha and Beta. Perhaps after you secure our systems from attack, you might look into that."

I meet Lukas' gaze. "Flash is right. We discussed the possibility of bringing our brothers in on our neuro-link. There have already been several moments when us being able to communicate telepathically would have been advantageous."

Lukas nods. "Agreed. After you secure your programming, you may look into extending your neuro-link to encompass Alpha and Beta."

"Thank you," Flash says, grinning at the man before looking expectantly at me.

I fight the urge to roll my eyes and follow his example instead. "Yes, thank you."

Lukas still doesn't look like he trusts me entirely, but I suppose his assessment is fair. Perhaps he's right and I don't know as much about being part of a warrior squad as I thought.

Tundra looks at the dead satyr and frowns. "Perhaps they came here to take out the other super soldiers, or perhaps they came to wipe out the Amberloq warriors completely, leaving Dornte defenseless."

Lukas pulls his datapad out of the thigh pocket of his black battle fatigues. "I'll tell Honor and Rhylan to tighten security and quietly lock down the castle until we know more. I'll also get him to allow Link access to the servers. In the meantime, I don't want anyone wandering the halls alone."

Tundra nods. "Return to your quarters and bunk up two or more to a room. Travel in pairs or groups when in the halls."

Lukas checks his watch. "We'll regroup for lunch at one. After we get the kids home, we'll be back out here pretending it's business as usual. On your toes, people. We've got ferrets in the henhouse."

～

Lark

LINK, Alpha, and Beta go with Lukas to find a secure computer terminal where Link can put his communication skills to use. He is tasked with closing whatever gap or loophole in their programming left them vulnerable to attack.

Tundra and Dune fly off to secure the site, check the wards, and review all security measures in case more of the Gen-3 soldiers are planning to attack from the outside.

That leaves Flash and me to find Yarko and mobilize him to get the kids back to Amberloq Hall.

As we walk the empty corridors, I fight the urge to slide my hand into his. He is my lover and our bond is growing with every touch and gaze that passes between us. Still, I'm here as an Amberloq Biome General observing the trials, and it's important that I look impartial.

I'm not sure I'm fooling anyone.

I'm truly falling for these guys.

Shift is contemplative and caring. Flash is loving and dedicated. There were even moments before our fight when Link betrayed his stoic broodiness to hand me something or help me with something or when he was playing pool with Skye. In those rare moments, I glimpsed the man afraid to risk himself.

It'll take time to undo what those scientist Brassholes did to them.

Ha! Brassholes. I love it.

And speaking of Brassholes, knowing there are enemies in our midst makes walking these halls an exercise in overcoming tension.

Every door and corner has become suspect.

Will someone jump out at us?

Will we be attacked if we're not paying attention?

Reaching out to Flash, I voice my concerns over the private channel Link established with me on that first day. *Do you think all of them are Gen-3 spies?*

There's no way to know. If we research them, they may have falsified files. If I touch them, I may or may not sense their intentions. They might have better programming than me, so they might be able to counter my abilities.

But you could tell with Kezay.

He was dead. There was no countering for him.

Good point. It's gratifying that the more time and intimacy shared between us, the easier it is to communicate with them like this.

It's like being part of something special.

As a person who was alone in the world even before the realm fell to chaos and so many people were lost, to truly belong to others and have them belong to me is an incredibly empowering thing.

I love you, Flash. I cast him a sideways glance and pull him into an alcove at the end of the hall. *When I saw Shift go down and then you fall next, my heart nearly froze in my chest. I realized then, I should've told you how I feel—how cherished you make me feel.*

Flash slides his hands around the back of my hips and pulls us body to body. Then, with a gentle finger under my chin, he lifts my mouth to his. *You are cherished, my lovely. From the moment we sat in the bunker interrogation room and you argued with Lukas to stay and answer our questions, you had my heart.*

Staring into those warm, golden eyes of his, how could I not fall for him? They built him to be the perfect soldier and the perfect man. Brass may think he created them, but the adaptations to their programming is no different from a child growing up with the ideas of their parents and then making their own choices.

It's a credit to his character that he chooses as well as he does. Honor. Compassion. Loyalty.

"I hate knowing Brass is coming after you," I say against his lips. "I need you with me so I can finally be happy and have a home."

Flash fingers a strand of my hair, creating a black coil along the digit. "You want that with me?"

"More than anything."

Dipping his head, he presses a kiss against my neck. The warmth of his lips on my flesh kicks my pulse up like it always does. This is what it feels like to be loved.

I feel his cock stirring against my thighs and wish we had the time and the privacy to explore this further. Breaking the kiss, I ease back and take a moment to catch my breath. "We have work to do, so this will have to wait. Still, I just wanted you to know."

His smile is sweet as he bites his bottom lip. "You wanted me to know what? Could you tell me again?"

I chuckle and give him another quick kiss. "I love you, Flash. You are the first man I've ever said those words to, so know how deeply true they are. I love you and want to stay with you."

"Then I will live to make that happen, my lovely. For your happiness is the only thing that fuels my bio-engineered soul. You are my catalyst and my love."

The two of us stand there, basking in our moment as the

reality of the realm moves on in the background of our lives. Eventually, the building sighs, we hear voices in the distance, and despite how it feels, we are not the only two people in the quadrant.

Flash slides his hand in mine and tugs me back into the hall. "First, we see the children safely away. Then we make do with whatever time we have left before we have to meet Lukas for the lunch meeting."

"Make do?"

He flashes me a sexy smile. "A delicious appetizer before the feast of a main course."

"I see. And what will you be consuming for your main course?"

The heated gaze he throws me draws a rush of damp heat to my core. "You, my lovely. I will feast on your body until I can't devour another bite."

Mmm... good answer.

CHAPTER NINETEEN

Mac

The dominance of my Sith side recedes slowly over the time I have Shift trapped in my room. Knowing he is here and safe does a lot to calm my cat. Knowing I've lain my claim, and he both accepted and welcomed my dominion, does even more.

"Mine," I whisper, the last of my energy draining.

The two of us lay strewn across my bed in a tangle of sheets and limbs. It's not the way I expected my day to go, but now that it's done, I can't imagine things ending up any other way.

Shift traces the tattoo fretwork decorating my torso and shoulder, studying the designs. He told me that first day we spent together that he wanted to suss out all their meanings.

That will take him a while.

Because as many designs as I have, they all have a story and a deep meaning for me. They each add a piece of information to the tale of who I am and how I became the man I am today.

"Do you regret it?" Shift asks, his whiskey-colored gaze

watching me. No doubt he's recording my response, so I want to get this right.

I roll back to get a better read on him.

Considering how sure he'd been the past week while he chased me down and tried to convince me I was his male, now that the deed is done, he doesn't look sure at all. "Do I regret claiming ye?"

He nods but says nothing.

"No. Why would ye think that?"

"You growled through most of the last hour. I worried your cat might have done something on an instinctual level that the man wouldn't want."

I shake my head. "Och, no. Don't think that. No, I don't regret a thing... except maybe not goin' with my instincts sooner and endin' that fucker before he grounded ye."

Damn, even thinking about that nearly liquifies my bowels.

"Then why were you growling?"

How do I explain this so it makes sense?

Propping myself up to sit, I pull a loose end of the sheet across my lap to keep focus. "Technically, my Sith cat and I are the same person, but in reality, there are moments when one or the other of us dominates. Usually, I'm the man driving the train... but today, it was definitely the cat who made the decisions."

His gaze narrows. "And even though your cat claimed me, you don't regret it?"

I hate the insecurity, but given the growling and my reaction in the beginning, I can't blame him. Reaching over his hips, I tug him closer. "No regrets, my sweet soldier boy. I remember the trainee takin' ye down, and then something inside me snapped and my instinct took over. I needed to get to ye."

"You the man or the cat?"

I take time to consider that. "Both. Yer my guy, right? The past few days should tell ye that much."

He offers me a hopeful nod. "But you didn't claim me until your cat took that choice away from you. I want to be sure because your anger before stemmed from being manipulated into feeling something you didn't choose to feel."

The sad longing in his voice is my fault and I know it. *Damn.* I thought we were past this. "Aye, I prefer to be in control of my choices—I won't deny that—but I don't feel like anything was taken from me. In fact, feeling like *you* were almost taken from me is what made everything fall into place."

I reach between us and brush my thumb across his cheek. "It took me a bit to wrap my head around it, but the truth is, we're bound. Fer better or worse, whatever comes, yer mine and I'm yers. The rest of it, we'll deal with together."

His expression brightens. "Lark warned me not to read too much into things. She said to wait until you told me how you feel about things or I might confuse an already confusing situation."

"Lark is a smart lass."

He props himself up and looks me over, his nose wrinkling at what he sees. "I think it's time I got you into the shower. Having sex with my lover while he's still wearing the blood of the man who attacked me was hot in the moment, but it's a little macabre now."

I glance down at myself and chuckle. "Agreed. Then lead the way, my sweet, and ye can clean me up."

Link

SITTING in front of the interface console, my knee bounces impatiently as my fingers tap on the keyboard. There is more access to the Amberloq databases from here than there was at the bunker. Then again, there weren't any official members of the Amberloq associated with the running of the bunker program except for Valorous Thornebane.

At the thought of that woman, the fury that simmers beneath the surface of my emotions threatens to break free. It was her idea to create us and then, when we didn't perform to her exact specifications on her exact timeline, she deemed us defective.

Because of that, we languished for twelve years in the dark void of nothingness, aware of our existence and of time passing, but unable to revive.

Yes, I'm angry, but I realize that taking my anger and mistrust out on the people here is an error.

Flash is right.

Lark has done nothing but try to help us.

Lukas has done nothing to earn my disrespect.

And I have done nothing to prove to them that putting their faith in us was the right course of action. Instead, I've made things more difficult for everyone.

I'm not sure if it's the reality that my brothers and I were defeated so easily today or Lukas and Dune's argument that I am a poor candidate to be part of a soldier squad, but something in my programming has shifted.

Dune said, *You don't know what you don't know.*

It sounds imbecilic, but I see his point.

On the first day of the trials, Lark said *a non-cohesive warrior, no matter his or her fighting skills, is more likely to get someone killed than help in a battle.*

She said they are looking for more than fighters.

And then, when all five of us were incapacitated in the blink of a moment, it was Mac who proved to be the warrior the situation needed.

Lukas' words replay in my mind next, *Being part of a warrior squad in the real world means the soldiers you serve with have different strengths. Someone might have experience with an enemy you haven't encountered, so you'll listen and consider their input.*

Another soldier might've grown up in the kind of climate or landscape you're about to infiltrate, so you accept their suggestions on approach or exfil. Their input is valuable and so you respect their place on your team.

I see his point. I may be a superior fighter, but there is more to being a soldier than my kill efficiency.

It's hard to believe that with my programming and intelligence, I could be so wrong about something, but I'm seeing it.

Yes, despite many people trying to tell me, now I understand.

Drawing a deep breath, I open the mental connection I share with Flash and Lark and brush their minds. I hope I am welcome and yet prepare myself that I might not be.

Flash responds without hesitation. *Brother? Is everything all right? Your emotional frequency feels off. Are you suffering ill effects from Kezay's sonic attack?*

No. I am well. I, uh... I wanted to apologize for my comments that night in our suite. I was acting under several misbeliefs and only now have I realized how skewed my thinking might have been.

Might? Lark repeats.

Apologies, Lady Lark. My frustrations and misgivings colored my perspective of things and I said things I regret.

Thank you, brother, Flash says, his relief rushing across our bond. *And I apologize for punching your stubborn, stupid face.*

I chuckle. *I suppose I deserve that.*

And more.

It hasn't escaped my attention that Lark has yet to respond. *Lady Lark? Will you accept my apology?*

There's a long silence when I don't feel her emotional energy over our neuro-connection at all. *I will consider it, Link. Saying you regret your actions is a good start, but I will hold my acceptance until I see if you mean it. You've been an insufferable, arrogant jerk and have offended more than just me. I look forward to seeing a more humble and agreeable side to you.*

Dune warned me that, given my comments, a mere apology wouldn't be enough. No matter, I will show her. *I accept your reservations and will mend what I have broken between us. You shall see.*

With that, I close the link and get back to my task at hand—directing my anger and hostility toward the one who truly deserves it—Andras Brass.

If he embedded a fatal flaw into our programming, I will find it. And in doing so, I will also search for any other design anomalies he may have threaded into our coding. I will not let him or his evil intentions take us down again. If he designed us to be shut down with a sonic or vibrational frequency, and he designed the Gen-3 soldiers to depend on one serum to keep them stable when another takes them out, there's no telling what other backdoor surprises he's set in place.

I write several sniffer programs to search through the databanks of the system and while they do their work, I go through every layer of file, through the accounting records, the communication records, the personal logs...

I go through everything Andras Brass ever wrote, typed, or did that I can trace.

My maker has met his match.

I will take him down.

Flash

THEY SAY that even in the darkest moments, there will be a light. Lark telling me she loves me an hour after being taken out on the training field is about the brightest, most brilliant light I can imagine. And then Link makes contact and apologizes? What? There is something truly unimaginable happening today...

And it's not even noon yet.

The two of us search the house, looking for Yarko to enlist him to take the Elbirfae kids home and out of the path of whatever nefarious plan the Gen-3 soldiers have put into motion.

Their failed attempt to take us down will force them to regroup and reassess. The lethal finality of Mac's response to Kezay's attack will give them pause.

At least it should... because wow, his cat really tore that man to shreds.

We arrive at the games room and find River and Danner hanging out with Stone and Storm.

"Hey, guys, do you know where Yarko is?" Lark's question is innocent enough, but the kids pick up on the tension in her voice immediately and straighten, looking alarmed.

"What's wrong? Is he in trouble?" Stone asks.

"Not at all. We need his portaling ability and I was hoping he was here."

They shake their heads. "Haven't seen him."

"Or Skye," Danner adds. "They're likely taking advantage of the training delay. Did you check their rooms?"

Lark nods. "Yeah, that's the first place we looked."

The contact of holding her hand allows me to sense the volatility in her emotions. She's getting worried.

"Hey, kids," I say, taking a shot at the whole guardian thing. "Considering what happened outside, how about you round up the others and stick together for a bit?"

River frowns. "Do you think Mac will hunt us down or something? He won't. You don't know him yet, but he's a good guy. That satyr was hurting Shift and his cat just got hissy, like Lukas said."

Lark shakes her head and steps inside the room, pulling the doors closed behind us. "It's not Mac we're worried about, guys. We think some very dangerous soldiers might've infiltrated our trials to kill Alpha, Beta, Flash, Shift, and Link."

Danner frowns. "Why? Are they jealous?"

"Who wouldn't be?" I say, lightening the mood.

Lark chuckles and rolls her eyes. "Really?"

I shrug. "I say we tell them."

"Tell us what?" River asks.

Lark steps to the side and gestures for me to take the floor. "It's your story to tell. If you want to tell them, that's your call."

So I do.

I tell them about Valorous' intention to create an army of elite soldiers and how Alpha and Beta were the prototypes of the first iteration and how my brothers and I were the second.

"And it's the third generation of super soldiers that are coming after you?" Storm asks.

"Yes. The Gen-3 soldiers aren't like the five of us. They are genetically enhanced fae hosts given bio-engineered strength and magical gifts."

"Why do they want to kill you?" Danner asks.

"Because our maker, Andras Brass, knows that we'll be coming after him and the five of us are the most threatening to his agenda."

"Now I'm even more glad Mac shredded that guy," Stone says.

The others nod their agreement.

"But we don't know who of the thirteen applicants that arrived this morning are genuine Amberloq warrior hopefuls and who are Gen-3 soldiers here to cause trouble."

"And that's why you need Yarko," Danner says. "You want him to take us home so you can sort through which of the people here are genetically modified assassins?"

I nod. "That's correct."

"But maybe we could help," River says. "There are twenty of us and a max of thirteen of them."

"Twelve now," Stone corrects.

"Right. Even better. It's twenty against twelve."

Lark shakes her head. "There is no scenario where I'm

keeping you kids here as part of the ruse to flush out enemy super soldiers."

Danner laughs. "Can you even believe you just said that out loud? It sounds crazy."

"Wait until Skye finds out," Stone says. "She thinks you guys are the coolest already. She'll go crazy when she hears this."

"Yarko and Skye already know," Lark says.

"And they didn't tell us?"

"They were told not to. Part of being a member of an elite policing force is understanding the importance of keeping tactical information quiet. We don't want it to be public knowledge that there are rogue automaton soldiers roaming the streets of Dornte under the control of a mad scientist."

Danner laughs again. "See, that's crazy talk."

It really does sound odd when she says it like that.

"So, round everyone up. Stay in groups and stay out of harm's way."

"Where do you want us?"

Lark looks at me, and I review the floor plan of the lodge in my mind. "There's a large library at the end of the hall on your floor. Get everyone and go there."

Lark nods. "We'll escort you to the bottom of the stairs. From there, you go straight up and get everyone together. If you find Yarko, tell him to take you all back to Amberloq Hall."

The boys nod. "Got it."

CHAPTER TWENTY

Mac

*a*s much as I would like to stay in my quarters for the rest of the day, once Shift and I finish in the shower, we towel off, get dressed and I resign myself to facing whatever clusterfuck arose from me killing one of the Amberloq trainees.

"You look worried," Shift says, taking a knee to tie up his boots.

"Had I been in my right mind, I would have only maimed the man for life, not shredded him."

"Does his death weigh on you?"

"No. It's not that. Whatever stunt the asshole was trying to pull, he miscalculated when he took my mate down with malice and intention."

Shift's smile warms my insides like my cat is stretching in the sun. "I enjoy being your mate."

The purr that rolls from the back of my throat is my cat's response. "That's a good thing because I intend to explore us bein' mates fer a good long time."

"It so happens, I am amenable to that."

The two of us are still chuckling about that as we stroll down the hall to the stairs and meet four of the kids rushing up like their asses are on fire. "What's the trouble, boys?"

It's one of the desert twins who speaks. "Lark told us what's happening. We're gathering everyone and getting ready to evacuate back to Amberloq Hall."

The hair on the back of my neck stands on end. "What's this now? What did Lark tell ye?"

They look at us, eyes wide.

It's River who speaks next. "That the Gen-3 soldiers have infiltrated the trials and are here to kill the five. We're supposed to round everyone up and wait for Yarko to portal us home before they take their next run at eliminating their super soldier competition."

I blink as all that sinks in. "So the fuckwad I slayed in the yard was a Gen-3?"

They all nod.

"Weel, that changes everything, doesn't it?"

River frowns. "You didn't know?"

I shake my head. "If ye remember, my cat was in a bit of a killin' frenzy. I didn't stop to consider the motivations of the man who just tried to kill my mate."

"Your mate?" Cue four pairs of curious eyes moving from me to Shift.

"I thought Shift was with Lark," Danner says, giving me a serious case of stink eye.

I wave away the hostility. "Nothin' is happenin' that ye need to concern yerselves with, kids. Shift and I and Lark and Flash… and even Link have things to sort out, but it's all good. I promise."

They don't look like they believe me, but I don't have time to explain our catalyst/bonded mate convoluted five-way to teenagers.

I can't even explain it to myself.

"All right. Do as Lark says and get yer friends and hunker down. Apparently, we have a little catchin' up to do. If ye run into any trouble, scream bloody murder. My cat will hear ye and we'll come runnin'."

The boys nod and rush off.

When it's just Shift and I again, I meet his gaze. "It seems we've missed quite a bit. We best get down there and find out what the feck is goin' on."

The two of us descend the stairs two at a time and when we get to the main floor, we hang a left and head straight for the war room.

"I hear I may have stirred up a hornet's nest," I say as we join Lukas, Dune, and Link.

"More like exposed it." Lukas casts a glance over his shoulder and meets my gaze. "You good?"

"Aye, never better."

Shift comes to stand beside me and Lukas' gaze slides from me to where the collar of his shirt has slid open and the tender pink flesh of my bite mark is exposed. "I see that."

I ignore the smug smirk and stay focused. "Tell me about the Gen-3 infestation. How did ye figure it out?"

Lukas tells us about Flash examining Kezay's corpse and him sensing the genetic modifications. "Once we knew that, him taking down the five like that made more sense. He knew what he was doing because he was programmed to do it."

"And do we know how many others there might be? Have we identified any of the other trainees?"

Dune shakes his head. "No. We've studied the security footage from when everyone got here and over the past three days. There's nothing obvious. Everyone has only spoken conversationally during meals and in the rec room or games room at night."

"There's no way they only sent one here," I say.

"Agreed," Lukas says.

"Do you think they know we brought the prisoners from the bunker here for interrogation?"

Lukas frowns and starts moving for the door. "If they do, they'll make a grab for them."

I follow him out and Shift and Dune take up the rear. The four of us jog out the door and run around the west end of the building.

Our path takes us past the helipad and that's when things go from bad to worse.

"Motherfucking assholes!" Lukas rushes over to where several of the mechanical panels for the helicopter are hanging open with cables cut and liquids pooling out onto the stone. "I really hate these guys."

"I'm with ye." I urge him past the carnage of our transportation and herd him back into motion. "Maybe we'll find a few at the prison cells and ye can light them up with yer fireballs."

"Promises, promises."

The four of us get going again. "Shift and Dune, fly on ahead. We'll be right behind ye."

Shift flashes me a scowl.

"It's cute that yer protective of me, soldier boy, but I'll be fine. Off ye go. If ye can catch up with the assholes, save one fer Lukas to blow up."

"Yes, please," Lukas grumbles.

The two of them fly up and over the building, but it doesn't do us any good. Because by the time we get around the west wing and into the containment area, Shift and Dune are coming back out.

"They're dead," Dune says.

"Dead? Do ye mean off-line?" I ask.

Dune shakes his head. "No. It looks like they were deemed a liability and someone ripped the primary data chips out of the base of their skull and also took something from their frontal cortex."

I sigh and shake my head. "I really feckin' hate these guys."

~

Lark

BY THE TIME Flash and I run into Mac and Shift, I'm losing my mind. The two of them are coming in from the front doors with Dune and Lukas. "Thank the powers we found you." And then I'm struck by the expressions on their faces. "What? What's happened?"

Shift rushes forward and hugs me. "Nothing that can't wait. Why do you look so distraught?"

"We can't find Yarko and Skye. We've searched everywhere we can without tipping our hands and there's no sign of them. Aside from knocking on the doors of the applicants that might well be Gen-3 soldiers, I don't know where they could be."

"So, ye haven't been able to get the kids portalled back to safety?" Mac asks.

"No. I planned for Yarko to do that." Lukas and Mac share a worried glance and the eels of anxiety twisting in my guts go wild. "What are you thinking?"

Mac frowns. "The helicopters were disabled."

"I don't follow. What does that—" It hits me then. "You think they've taken Yarko so we can't leave?"

Flash shakes his head. "But between the Elbirfae and us, almost everyone can fly. We can still evacuate and carry those who don't have wings."

"But we don't know which of the applicants are Gen-3 and which are innocents here for a chance to become Amberloq," Lukas says. "And we can't leave and abandon prospective warriors because we're unsure."

"The kids could fly off though," I say. "At least then, there would be fewer innocents for us to worry about."

Flash nods, and a rush of relief replaces my panic. "If we can get the kids away from this, we can continue to search for Yarko and Skye without worrying about more of them being in danger."

"What do you mean, search for Skye?" Tundra says, striding up the hall with Link, Alpha and Beta. "Where's Skye? What happened?"

Lukas strides forward and stops before him, grabbing his shoulders. "We don't know anything for sure, Ice Man. Lark and Flash have been searching for Yarko to get the kids back to Amberloq Hall, and none of them know where Skye and Yarko are. They could've just snuck off somewhere for privacy. We don't know anything."

Lukas' reassurances aren't exactly accurate... unless Yarko and Skye are spending their private time with the other applicants.

"The point is, the kids can fly back to Thornebane Castle on their own and we can deal with what's happening here."

"No, they can't," Tundra says, frowning. "That's why I came to find you. I went to check the security wards, and they'd been tampered with. I don't know enough about the magic Valorous had cast over this place, so I need you to come help me figure out what's been done. But if Skye's missing—"

"—We don't know that."

Tundra is a big man and I've seen him face off against armed brutes and terrorists to the quadrant and this is the first time I've ever seen fear in his eyes.

"They're smart kids," I say, trying to help. "And we think they're together, so there's that."

Dune nods. "And there's no way Yarko will let anything happen to her. Skye is the air he breathes. Even if they're in trouble, the moment he can portal, he'll get her somewhere safe."

Tundra nods. "Yeah, he will, but what if he can't portal?"

Lukas waves away his words. "We can't start speculating. We need to deal with what we know for sure. The two of us will go check out the security wards. You can explain to me how they work and I will try to figure out what they've done to alter them. Lark, you and Shift go make sure the kids are secure. Mac, Flash, and Dune, I want you to knock on doors and interview the applicants one by one. Mac knows the questions to ask. Flash, you need to touch them and see if your gift can pick up anything to tell us whether they're spies, and Dune will watch to intercede if they make an aggressive move. We've got twelve possible hostiles, so be careful."

"What do you want us to do?" Alpha asks, gesturing to Beta and Link.

"You three will go back to the war room and try to get word to Honor or Rhylan at Amberloq command. Link, you're our communications guy. Do your best to let them know we're pinned down. Then, start patrolling the halls and see if anyone is where they shouldn't be. No one goes anywhere alone, got it? We're on a buddy system until this shit show is sorted out."

The male grunts and head nods signal that everyone agrees.

Shift moves to my side and presses a hand at the small of my back. Even so, his gaze is squarely on Mac. "Strength to you. Be well."

Mac winks at him. "Don't look so worried, soldier boy. I've been in much bigger scrapes than this. I'll see ye soon."

"Do you swear?"

He nods. "Oh, yeah. I swear."

With that, our group breaks up and everyone heads off to follow Lukas' orders.

CHAPTER TWENTY-ONE

Link

The moment Alpha, Beta, and I arrive back at the war room, it's obvious it will be a futile effort to notify Princess Honor of our current situation. Not only is the door unlocked, it's physically off the hinges and hanging at an awkward angle.

The three of us are on high alert immediately.

I rush to the door and head inside. "The two of you guard the door while I assess the damage to the communication system—"

The hit comes fast and low.

My boots find no purchase as two hundred and fifty pounds of warrior hits me like a freight conveyance. Flying sideways, I eject my wings and twist to see where he's taking me.

My shirt offers only the slightest resistance before the fabric shreds and my wings flair out behind me. The momentum of the tackle takes us both careening over the surface of the digital war table and down onto the hard floor beyond.

Despite the suddenness of the attack, I use the blade-sharp

edge of my wing to slice the arm still grappling me around the chest.

The soldier's wail makes me smile as I grip his head and twist. It would be my greatest pleasure to rip his head free from his neck, but unfortunately, he's made sturdier than that.

I have to content myself with getting free from his hold and clocking him again. Movement to my right has me spinning for a second incoming attack.

Either we've surprised these men during their subterfuges or they knew we would come to secure the communications and were lying in wait.

Alpha is at my side a moment later and when a staggering roundhouse kick to my hip knocks me toward the weapon's cabinet, I see Beta battling in the hall. A blow to my temple has my ocular stabilization refocusing and in the time I take to stand, I've got one soldier coming at me from the front, and another from behind.

"Hold him so I can do this," the one in the back says. It's the one who first attacked me, and I'm happy to see the gash in his arm is bleeding profusely.

When he raises his hands, the glint of the metal tool in his grasp makes my blood run hot. It's the device Brass' scientists used to access the data chips at the back of our necks.

I have a good idea what these men intend to do to me, and I'm not keen on being decommissioned today.

I lunge with all my weight, grabbing the tool and striking out with my wings to hold back his partner. His hands are slick with blood, and I use that to my advantage.

Gripping the tool, I pull it lower. If it goes into my side or my chest, it's simply a blade puncturing my body. If it goes into my neck, I will be disabled.

The steel penetrates the muscle below my ribs and the burn of torn flesh ramps my incentive to kill. The tidal wave of sweet-fire anger I hold back is finally free and directed at someone worthy.

Andras Brass and his scientists would be better.

One of his minions will have to do.

With a lethal force honed to precision, I leverage my weight and spin. The sharp edge of my wings catches the one in front of me unprepared, and his severed head falls to the ground with a mighty *thunk.*

That evens the odds to one-on-one.

Yanking the metal access tool from my side, I bend it in on itself and throw it across the floor and under the closet doors. With that taken care of, I test the gash on my side with my fingers.

The puncture is two inches above my hip and stings badly. No vital organs were hit.

I'll deal with that later.

The moment Beta's opponent drops, he straightens and my second attacker seems to realize it's now two on one in favor of the good guys.

He's across the room, throwing the mangled door into our path, and sprinting down the corridor in the next racing heart beat.

It takes a moment for Beta and I to get around the damaged door, but we're only seconds behind him.

Up ahead, and unseen by Alpha, my fleeing attacker launches high in the air and comes down hard with an elbow from behind. The brutal strike knocks our brother to the ground, unconscious. The two of them grab Alpha, one under each of his arms, and run.

"Alpha is in trouble," I shout over my shoulder. "Hurry, Beta. We must help him before they rip his data chip out."

I don't wait for a response. It strikes me a moment too late that this could be them luring us into a trap, but there's no help-ing it.

I'm in pursuit.

Mac

FLASH, Dune and I finish speaking with Alryx-Ti and I'm relieved the mountain elf seems to be a genuine warrior hopeful and not a Gen-3 soldier... because holy hell, he's as big as a mountain and is one of the fiercest applicants here.

I was not looking forward to taking him down.

Thankfully, there was no need. He gave off no scents of deception while I interrogated him. He allowed Flash to touch him and read his intentions. And when Dune asked him to lift his hair and let me examine the back of his neck for a data chip access port, he did so without hesitation.

All good signs.

"The room's clear too."

It's both good and bad that we didn't find Yarko and Skye here... but mostly good. "Thanks so much, lad, and again, I'm sorry to have to question ye."

The elf shrugs. "I assume this has something to do with Kezay's attack this morning."

"Aye, it does."

He shrugs. "Well, if hostiles are here, you have to do what is necessary to satisfy your safety checks. I am fine with that, as I have nothing to hide."

I nod and gesture for the other two to head toward the door. "That's good of ye to say. We'll get this cleared up as quickly as we can, but until then, I have to ask ye to stay in yer room, so ye don't get caught in the crossfire if things go badly."

"Or I could help. If you tell me a bit more about who or what you are looking for, I can be another set of eyes and ears." He gestures to the long, pointed ears that extend so far off his head that they rise above the top of his silver hair. "I have great ears."

I chuckle. "Aye, ye do, and we appreciate the offer, but the fewer movin' parts we have on this one, the better. Stay here and we'll get things sorted as quickly as possible."

He nods. "Very well. If you change your mind, you know where I am."

"Done deal, thanks."

"Thanks, man," Dune says, clasping hands with him as we exit. "And make sure you lock up when you close the door."

When the *click* of the lock sounds, the three of us move to the door across the hall and down one.

We told the applicants to claim a room on this floor by closing the door, so thankfully, we don't have to check all the bedrooms because most of them still have their doors open.

Dune knocks on the next door. "Hey, there, it's Dune. Can I speak to you a moment?"

When no one answers, I get a bad feeling. "We told everyone to go back to their rooms, so whoever claimed this room should be inside."

"Unless they are busy disabling helicopters and killing prisoners," Dune says.

"Or this could be Kezay's room," Flash adds.

"Both are possibilities," I say.

Dune knocks again and then grips the handle of the door. I nod and take a step back, so I can see into the room. "Ready."

He turns the handle and swings the door inward, stepping inside in a rush with me right behind him, gun drawn. I pan the aim of my sidearm around the room and follow Dune as he opens the closet door and the small bathroom.

"Clear." Dune sets the curtain of the bathtub back into place and comes back to join us.

Flash has a nondescript duffel sitting on the bed and is

pulling out its contents. "A pair of pants. Two shirts. And a map of this compound."

Dune frowns, grabbing the folded paper and studying in. "Yep, and it's got the war room and the prison cell access door labeled."

"But this isn't Kezay's room," Flash says, shaking first the pants and then the t-shirts out and holding them out for us to examine. "Kezay was tall and wiry and had furred legs. He didn't wear pants like this and this shirt wouldn't even reach his waist."

I nod. "Yer right. So, whose room is this and where is our short and skinny little trouble-maker?"

There's no way to answer that at the moment.

The three of us leave the bag unpacked and the door open. There's no need to pretend we weren't in there because this whole infiltration is busted and they certainly aren't trying to stay under the radar.

Dune moves to the next door down the hall and knocks. "Hey, there, it's Dune. Can I speak to you a moment?"

When nobody answers, we go through the same routine. Dune grabs the door handle and looks over at me. I raise my gun, take a step back, and nod.

The inhale I take isn't a conscious action to test the air, but the moment the smell hits my sinuses, I curse and dive to stop Dune from opening that door.

I'm too late.

There's no stopping the bomb from going off.

Shift

LARK AND I head upstairs while the others break off on their tasks. I dislike the idea of Mac and Flash seeking the enemy.

Link is tasked with the communications system the enemy won't want us to have access to. Alpha and Beta will watch for hostiles in the halls and haven't been out of stasis long enough to assess the warriors they come across. The young Elbirfae are at risk, and Skye and Yarko are missing.

"Are you all right?" Lark casts me a sideways glance as we jog up the stairs.

"The situation concerns me on multiple levels. Caring for people and worrying for their safety is very distracting."

When we crest the top step on the third floor, she squeezes my arm. "It can be. I'm sure it's even more overwhelming because the onslaught of emotions is still new to you. Try to compartmentalize it."

"What do you mean?"

"Ask yourself, what outcomes can you affect? What do you have control over? Focus your energy on those things and trust everyone else to do the same."

"I'm uncertain it makes me feel any better."

She smiles. "Your brothers are smart and capable. Mac is a brilliant soldier and with his cat, he's a fearsome warrior. Trust that they will do what needs to be done to survive and thrive."

I rub at the tension in my chest. "Your advice is sound, but the tension I feel is unaffected."

"Well, if your emotions are still effecting you, can you turn them down a bit?"

I consider her question. "Yes, I could, although I'm unsure that will be necessary. I don't believe my concerns will affect my performance should trouble arise."

She hugs me for a moment and then eases back. "You know best. Come on. Let's check on the kids."

The two of us stride down to a grand library at the end of the third-floor corridor. The doors are closed and no sound is leaking through to the hall, but Lark said this is where she sent them.

"Knock, knock," she whispers, leaning close to the seam of the double doors. "Guys, it's me and Shift. Let us in."

The door opens almost immediately and we slide inside to speak with them.

"Is everyone all right in here?" she asks.

River steps forward, looking concerned. "Have you found Yarko and Skye?"

"No. Not yet."

"We've been talking," Stone says. "We think we should help you look. They've got to be here somewhere and if the Gen-3 soldiers have done something to them, they might need our help."

Lark shakes her head. "Flash and I searched the entire place. Other than the bedrooms of the applicants, there is nowhere we haven't looked."

"Then we need to check their rooms," River says.

I nod. "We are. Mac, Flash, and Dune are going door to door. If Yarko and Skye are being detained, they'll find them."

"Then what can we do?" Storm asks.

"You can stay here and stay safe. With Yarko missing and the helicopter disabled, there's nothing for you to do but avoid being taken or hurt by the Gen-3 soldiers."

Danner frowns. "You think they'll come after us?"

I shake my head. "I doubt it. They've come here for me and my brothers. If you stay out of their way, you should draw no interest from them."

"But we *want* to help. We're here to become Amberloq warriors so that we can protect our quadrant. We should stand up to them and prove ourselves."

When a rowdy surge of agreement breaks from the group, I hold up my hands. "In theory, perhaps. The truth is, as of right now, you're unequipped to take on the level of opposition these foes possess."

"Then give us something we can use against them," River says.

Lark shakes her head. "The weapons we confiscated with the takedown serum are at Thornebane Castle. Lukas left them with Honor a few nights ago for our scientists to study. Truly, the best thing you can do to help us is to—"

The thundering boom downstairs stops all conversation. The floor quakes beneath our feet, and then the doors explode open. A massive wave of detonation and fire throws Lark and me hurtling through the air.

The force of the blast knocks my systems offline and everything goes dark.

Thank you for reading Rise from Ruin, book two of Lark's trilogy. I hope you enjoyed getting to know Mac a little better and seeing how things unfold with Lark, Flash, Shift, and Link. While the story is fresh in your mind, and as a favor to me, please leave a review and tell other readers what you thought. A quick star rating and/or even one sentence can mean so much to readers deciding whether to try a book, series, or a new-to-them author.

Thank you.

And if you enjoyed it, continue with the ultimate book in both Lark's love story, and the Guardians of the Fae Realms series book 15—Trust and Triumph.

ABOUT THE AUTHOR

Author Notes

Written on 03/15/2023

I hope you enjoyed Rise from Ruin, book 14 of the Guardians of the Fae Realms series and the second book in the trilogy of Lark's harem.

With only one book left in the series, I've been thinking about everything that has happened in this series over the past couple of years.

It's been a fun ride.

I owe you a couple of bonus scenes—my apologies. I haven't forgotten and will catch up at some point soon.

I hope you're enjoying the dynamic of Lark, Mac, Shift, Flash, and Link. Don't forget to grab Trust and Triumph and follow the five as they rebuild the Amberloq forces and secure Dornte.

Thank you for reading, and for making it all the way through this series.

JL

The Amberloq face their greatest fears to secure the Crown of Dornte.

Valorous Thornebane might have envisioned her genetically engineered soldier program being the best way to secure the Crown of Dornte, but when Andras Brass sold out and redirected the army against them, that all changed.

Now, instead of protecting Dornte, Gen-3 soldiers threaten to undermine everything they're trying to rebuild in the quadrant.

With the financial backing of greedy citizens funding their treachery, Lark and her mates must rebuild the Amberloq force and eliminate the threat once and for all.

Their quint is set. The Amberloq forces are ready. The final battle has begun.

Find Me

My Direct Sales Site: Shopify

My books

Web page – www.jlmadore.com

Email – jlmadorewrites@gmail.com

Discord— https://discord.gg/uwgngKeF3a

Newsletter – JL Series Updates

ALSO BY JL MADORE

Book 1 – Captured by the Magi

Book 2 – Jesse and the Magi Vault

Book 3 – The Makings of a Magi Knight

Book 4 – Clash with the Magi Council

Book 5 – The Unstoppable Storme

Club Sanguine

Book 1 – Moonstone Maelstrom

Book 2 - Sunstone Sacrifice

JL's More Traditional M/F, M/M, or Menage

The Watchers of the Gray Series (Paranormal)

Book 1 – Watcher Untethered – Zander

Book 2 – Watcher Redeemed – Kyrian

Book 3 – Watcher Reborn – Danel

Book 4 – Watcher Divided – Phoenix

Book 5 – Watcher United – Seth

Book 6 – Watcher Compelled – Bo

Book 7 – Watcher Unfeigned – Brennus

Book 8 – Watcher Exposed – Taharqa

The Scourge Survivor Series (Fantasy)

Book 1 – Blaze Ignites

Book 2 – Ursa Unearthed

Book 3 – Torrent of Tears

Book 4 – Blind Spirit

Book 5 – Fate's Journey

Book 6 – Savage Love – epilogue novella

Aliens of Atlantis Series (Sci-Fi)

Book 1 – Taryn's Tiderider

Book 2 – Kai's Captive

Book 3 – Alyandra's Shadow